THE
LAST SIEGE

JONATHAN STROUD

MIRAMAX BOOKS
HYPERION PAPERBACKS FOR CHILDREN
New York

Copyright © 2003 by Jonathan Stroud
All rights reserved. No part of this book may be reproduced or transmitted in any form or by any means, electronic or mechanical, including photocopying, recording, or by any information storage and retrieval system, without written permission from the publisher. For information address Hyperion Books for Children, 114 Fifth Avenue, New York, New York 10011-5690.

Originally published in the United Kingdom by Random House Children's Books. Reprinted by permission.

First U.S. paperback edition, 2006
1 3 5 7 9 10 8 6 4 2
This book is set in 12-point Bembo.
Printed in the United States of America
ISBN 1-4231-0107-3

Library of Congress Cataloging-in-Publication data on file.
Visit www.hyperionbooksforchildren.com

For Eli and Matt

GROUND FLOOR

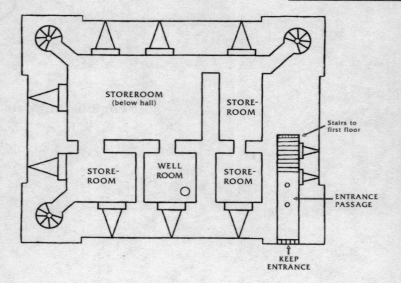

STOREROOM
(below hall)

STORE-ROOM

STORE-ROOM

WELL ROOM

STORE-ROOM

Stairs to first floor

ENTRANCE PASSAGE

KEEP ENTRANCE

FIRST FLOOR

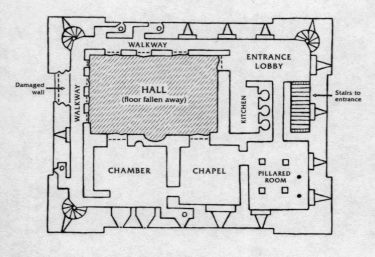

WALKWAY

ENTRANCE LOBBY

Damaged wall

WALKWAY

HALL
(floor fallen away)

KITCHEN

Stairs to entrance

CHAMBER

CHAPEL

PILLARED ROOM

KEY:

Spiral stair

I--‑I Railings or netting

Steps

Window

PLAN

SECOND FLOOR

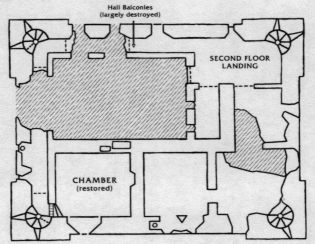

Hall Balconies
(largely destroyed)

SECOND FLOOR
LANDING

CHAMBER
(restored)

TOWER LEVEL

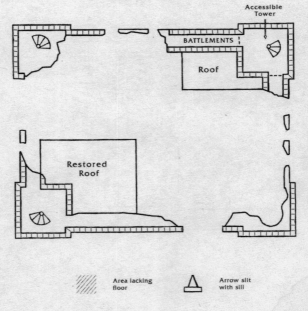

Accessible
Tower

BATTLEMENTS

Roof

Restored
Roof

Area lacking
floor

Arrow slit
with sill

Door

SKIRMISHES

1

Emily's first crime was a small one caused by snow.

Roots tripped her; her boots plunged into drifts. Tiny powder avalanches cascaded coldly onto her hat, brow, and shoulders. Little by little, she squeezed herself through the gap in the thick hedge, the snow-covered twigs butting and scraping against her anorak. Flakes landed on her eyelids and made her blink. Behind her, the sled caught against something. She yanked viciously at the cord and felt it bump itself free.

With another step she was standing in the castle grounds, her heart beating fast, her eyes peeled for danger. So far, so good. There was no one in sight.

She was up to her knees in a low drift that had built up inside the hedge. Away to the right, a straggling flock of birds flew in the gray sky above the woods, while the far hedge was a charcoal line drawn unevenly against the whiteness. All the small dips of Castle Field had been smoothed away by the snow, but a deep shadow beyond marked the great curve of the moat ditch. A few patches of broken wall leaned out drunkenly from the moat's raised inner lip.

In the background the body of the keep itself rose like a black slab.

Turning, Emily hauled on the cord. Abruptly the sled jerked into view, only to jam again behind the final mess of stems and tangled thorn. She bent down and pulled the yellow plastic, twisting it so that it came clear. Then she guided it out of the hedge and let it fall onto the drift.

She listened. Echoing laughter came from the direction of the moat, muffled by distance and the blanketing snow. Good, others were trespassing, too, and no one had come to catch *them*. It was going to be all right.

She set off across the field, each stride flaking her legs with white. The cold prickled through her jeans. Later it might become damp and chafing, but now it invigorated her. Every step helped freeze away the indoor stuffiness of the last few days.

She went down into a slight dip. Now she could no longer see the keep, just part of the outer wall, gray, crested with ice. The sky was heavy with the next snow. Her breath rose in ragged bursts of cloud.

The voices came from the steepest part of the moat, and Emily slowly made her way toward them. It all depended on who it was. Karen had said she might go sometime that week, and Emily quite liked Karen. If she was there, Emily would stay. If not . . .

A group of people clambered from the moat, dragging a small red sled. Two girls and four boys—all slipping and swearing and breathing hard. Their clothes were half caked with snow. Karen was not among them.

When all were at the top, three of the boys immediately began to push each other playfully at the edge of the moat. They uttered loud cries as they wrestled, hoping to gain the attention of the girls, who ignored them completely as they watched the fourth (and biggest) boy putting the sled in position. One girl flopped onto the sled, the other squeezed awkwardly on behind, and the biggest boy flung himself across the front girl's lap to a chorus of delighted shrieks and groans. The sled inched slowly down the slope, and braked almost to a standstill by a mess of protruding legs and arms. All at once the boy and the girl at the front tumbled off and the remaining rider shot down the rest of the way, whooping with terror, until she went headfirst into a drift at the bottom. The other boys had been wrestling with less enthusiasm; they now broke off and began laughing enviously at the biggest boy, who was lying on top of the girl halfway down the slope.

Deirdre Pollard, Katie Fern, the Allen brothers. Emily curled her lip and turned away. She would sled on her own. Deirdre and Katie were stupid, and the Allens had a bad reputation. Only the youngest, Simon, was still at school; the others hung about the village, aggressively doing nothing. Martin Allen, the eldest, had been the most aggressive of all, but he hadn't been seen for a while. Emily had heard he was in prison.

When she had got a good way from the group, she stopped, positioned her sled on the top of the slope, and sat. Below her was a steep chute of white treachery, all its rocks and holes cloaked from sight. Emily paused, clenched her teeth, and pushed off.

A spray of sleet, a funnel of cold air, a juddering whirl of whiteness. Then she was leveling out and coming to rest against the bottom of the opposite slope, her body jerking forward, her outstretched boots scrunching into the snow.

Standstill. It had taken all of three seconds.

Emily sat there catching her breath, grinning with the adrenaline.

Then something hit her in the face.

It snapped her head to one side, ripping out a gasp

as the thin cold pain tore across her cheek. The suddenness confused her. She knew it was a snowball, but it felt like the blow of a fist.

Loud laughter. Something else whistled in front of her face. Another missile hit her leg, shattering snow shards into her eyes.

Emily struggled to her feet, tripping over the sled cord, half blinded with tears from the impact. As if through wet glass, she saw her attackers a little way off along the bottom of the moat. Snowballs scudded through the air; a couple struck her chest and stomach. She bent for the cord, turned, and started to stumble away through the drifts.

She skidded, almost fell, righted herself—then there was a tremendous clout on the back of her head, her hat fell off in a shower of ice particles, and she knew she was about to cry.

She ran on, leaving the hat behind. It was impossible to go fast—the snow was too deep—but slowly the fusillade thinned and the jeers grew fainter. Another missile hit her on the leg, another shot past her ear, then the attack ceased.

Emily continued along the bottom of the moat, crying a little with misery and rage. At last she risked a look behind her, and saw that the curve of the slope had carried her out of view.

She slowed to a trudge. On either side, the slope was too steep to climb, but she knew if she continued she would come to the place where steps cut in the grass led up to the bridge. Then she could make her way back to the hedge and go home.

A fragment of the outer wall rose from the snow at the top of the right-hand bank. Emily wished she could push it down on the fools who had attacked her. She had stopped crying now and was kicking the snow savagely with every step. Katie Fern, Deirdre Pollard—she'd get back at them, see if she wouldn't. But there was nothing she could ever do about the boys—they were just too big, even that gormless Simon.

She hated them! She hated the whole village! Everyone there was stupid and brainless, and she was always left on her own with nothing to do. Sledding was the only possible way to stave off the Christmas boredom—and now she was getting beaten up for doing it! She couldn't go anywhere else, either. For twenty miles in all directions the land was flat—an endless boring tablecloth of gray-white fields, scored with ice-choked ditches, runs, and rivulets. Mud and water everywhere and not a slope in sight. The castle moat was the *only* place to take your sled, and now she was being driven away from it, back to her dull house, her dull parents—

She was so caught up in her fury and despair that she failed to see the figure before she was almost upon him. A sudden movement made her look up. A boy she did not know was standing ahead of her at the bottom of the moat.

He looked a little older than she, fifteen or so, thin, with a mop of black hair protruding from all sides of a dark blue bobble hat. A blue anorak protected him from the cold, but he also wore trainers, which Emily knew must be soaked right through. And he had no gloves. He was scraping up snowballs, compacting them hard with his bare hands, and throwing them up at the ruined wall on the top of the rise. Each ball hit against the stonework or vanished with a slight sound into the snow at its base. There was no one standing on the wall that Emily could see. The boy was alone.

Emily stood watching him. He made no sign that he had seen her, but stooped to gather up another handful of snow. He threw it, as hard as he could, then made a little noise of disapproval as it spattered into the top of the slope.

His hands were red with cold.

"You're trying to get them over the top?" Emily asked.

The boy did not turn to look at her. "Yes."

"It's very high."

"I've done it once, but my arms are getting tired now."

"Why don't you stop, then?"

The boy didn't answer, but packed another snowball between his freezing fingers and threw. It plopped half-heartedly midway up the slope.

"I'd stop if I were you," Emily said.

"What I need is a siege engine," declared the boy, brushing his hands on his front and stuffing them into his coat pockets. "You know, a massive catapult. I could do it from miles off, then."

"Do what?"

"Chuck rocks onto the defenders. Or burning lumps of pitch to set the place on fire. That would be the *best* way of doing it."

Emily looked at the boy. He had a longish, serious face, with pale skin and dark eyes that flicked rapidly back and forth between her and the wall above.

"I thought castles were made of stone," she pointed out helpfully. "Fire wouldn't do anything."

"A lot of the outer buildings were wooden," the boy replied. "But, yeah, you're right. Fire wouldn't do much apart from fry a few defenders. Of course," he went on, "the other option would be heads."

"Heads?"

"Of the enemy. Soldiers killed in forays, or local

villagers. We'd chop off their heads and lob them back over the wall so that they rained down on their families and friends. Psychological warfare."

"I'd stick to snowballs," Emily said.

There was a silence. "You from round here, then?" the boy asked finally.

"From the village. You?"

"I cycled from King's Lynn. Only took me half an hour."

"Where's your bike, then?"

"I left it in the dip by the hedge."

"Oh." This seemed to have exhausted the conversation. Emily could see the steps leading out of the moat up ahead. She started off.

"Don't you like castles?" the boy said suddenly.

"Yes, but right now I'm cold. I need to move about."

"They're the best. Each one's different. They had to keep changing their ideas, you see, because of all the military developments. This one's an early one, of course."

"Is it?" Emily shifted from one foot to the other, but it seemed rude to walk off while the boy was waffling.

"You can tell that 'cause of the keep. Later on they didn't bother with keeps. They were strong, but much too cramped. And if they had square corners, they were always getting undermined. You know, tunneling."

"This one hasn't been," Emily said, feeling a certain local pride.

"I know. Look at these outer walls, though. Someone's blown them to pieces. Who did it?" He asked the question directly, expecting an answer.

"No idea."

"Oh." The boy said this in a disappointed way that slightly annoyed Emily. "Some of these armies had great siege engines," he went on. "But you don't always need to destroy the walls. You know the Mongols? They were besieging some Christian castle. In Turkey, I think. Couldn't get in. So do you know what they did?"

"No."

"They got some bodies of Mongol soldiers who'd died of plague. Black boils all over them. Waited till they were really festering, ready to pop—"

He paused for a second, as if hoping Emily would say something. She didn't.

"—then they catapulted the bodies over the walls into the city. Pretty soon the defenders started to get poxy themselves. The plague spread and they were trapped in with it. Couldn't escape. Most of them died. Then the Mongols went off. They hadn't got inside the castle, but why should they care? They'd got their horrible revenge!"

"That's foul." Emily screwed up her face to prove it. She was impressed. The boy grinned.

"And when the Christian survivors went back to Europe, they brought the plague with them. That's how it got here. Spread everywhere. All because of siege warfare."

"How do you know that?" Emily asked.

"Read it somewhere." He lobbed another snowball. It arced lazily into the snow. "Don't you read?"

"Yeah, but not that sort of stuff."

"You've just got to look out for it. I've a good memory for that kind of thing."

Emily shrugged. The wind had picked up, and even at the bottom of the sheltered moat she could feel it cutting through her clothes. "Well," she said finally, "I'm going home. We shouldn't be here, anyway."

"That's part of the fun, isn't it?" The boy appraised her with a quick look. "Listen, before you go, why don't you chuck around some snowballs with me? You'll warm up then. You can be the defender. Or the attacker, if you want, though defending will be easier. You can be up there, by that hole—"

"No, thanks. I've had enough of snowballs for one day."

The boy looked crestfallen. "Suit yourself. Bet it would be good fun, though. You could chuck down boiling oil on me—you know, scoop up great handfuls of snow and just chuck it! If I was caught in it you'd win. Then we'd swap."

Emily considered. She really didn't want another snowball fight, but despite herself, the boy's enthusiasm was catching. It seemed a better option than slinking away on her own. Besides, pelting him with snow was a good opportunity to let off some of her pent-up rage.

"What's your name?" she asked.

"Marcus. Yours?"

"Em. So, how am I going to get up, then?"

The boy's face brightened. "Great! Yeah, it's a bit steep here, but there are some steps a bit farther along. That's how I got down."

Emily frowned. "I'm not trekking all that way. I'll climb it."

But Emily had hardly started up the slope when she heard footsteps crunching the snow behind her. She dropped back down and looked. A boy was approaching along the bottom of the moat.

Emily's eyes narrowed. It was Simon Allen, and he was carrying her hat.

She turned to face him, glaring stonily, arms rigid at her side. The boy was red-faced and discomforted. He came to a halt in front of Emily and stood there, gazing fixedly at an unexciting patch of snow by her feet. Emily said nothing. She could see Marcus looking from one of them to the other and back again.

Simon Allen held out the hat. Emily stepped forward and took it, almost snatching it out of his hands. She didn't put it on, but returned her arms to her sides and forced herself to look at the boy's face.

Like his brothers, he was big-framed, almost as tall as a man, though he was only in the year above Emily. Unlike his brothers, he had not yet gained too much weight—he was still quite slim, and his arms and legs seemed slightly gawky, a little too long for him. He had sandy hair cut short all over, a red, freckled face, and blue eyes. At this moment his mouth was hanging open a little as he struggled for something to say. Emily waited, looking at him.

At last the mouth opened decisively. "I found it," he said. "I—I thought it was your hat."

"It *is* my hat," Emily said. "That's why I took it. I don't steal things." She paused deliberately. "Unlike some people."

The boy flushed and clenched his fists. "Meaning what?"

Emily grinned. "Didn't see your big brother with you just now. Enjoying Christmas, is he?"

"You cow—you take that back!"

"Get lost."

Simon Allen made a move forward. Emily sneered at him, though her heart jolted with fear. "That's right. Beat up a girl. Twice in one morning's good going."

The boy stopped still, his mouth twisted with fury. "Listen, you bloody cow," he said, "I came to find you, to say sorry and give you your hat——"

"Well, why didn't you?"

"What?"

"Say sorry, you berk."

"I—I . . ." The boy seemed torn between perplexed confusion and inarticulate wrath. As he stood there spluttering, Marcus said, "What did he do?"

"Threw snowballs at me. They really hurt."

Simon Allen looked up. "I didn't throw any. It was the others."

"Oh, right, like you didn't."

"I bloody didn't! Well, I threw one, but it missed. It was Carl who hit you most."

"So you're a lousy shot. That makes all the difference."

"Look," said Marcus, interrupting just as Simon was about to explode with fury, "I've got a suggestion. Why doesn't he apologize and you accept it and then both of you just shut up? Then we can have a *fair* fight. Like we were going to, but with two attackers—I reckon the defender's got it easy else. Two attackers would balance things out. What about him defending and you and me attacking? That would be fairer. Then you both get a chance to pelt each other's brains out, anyway."

Emily and Simon Allen looked at Marcus dumbly. Emily was so amazed by his interruption that she had lost track of the argument, and though the last thing in the world she wanted was to have anything to do with Simon, when she tried to voice her objections, they seemed somehow petty and foolish. It was clear that much the same thing had happened to Simon. He coughed and dropped his gaze to the snow again.

"Well," he said in a mumble, "I'm sorry about the snowballs."

". . . That's okay." Emily could barely force it out.

Marcus grinned. "Great! Let's get on with it. You get up the slope, mate, and—" He stopped short. "Who's this lot? More volunteers?"

Emily looked, her heart sinking. Five figures, five grinning faces were approaching along the bottom of the moat. Katie Fern, Deirdre Pollard, the three brothers.

"Like a highway, this moat," Marcus said.

The biggest brother spoke. "We lost you, Si," he said. "Bit worried. Didn't know where you'd got to."

"Well, now you've found me," Simon said sulkily. "Not much to see, is there?"

"What you doing slipping off here? Made some new little friends?"

"Leave it, Carl." Simon's voice was wearily defiant.

"Maybe we're not good enough for you?"

"*Leave* it. I'm not doing anything."

Katie Fern pointed at Emily's sled. "He was going to sled," she said.

Carl whistled. "In *that* thing?"

"I wasn't, I wasn't going to sled."

"Bleeding toy sled, that is," Carl said. He laughed, triggering an instant echoing giggle from the two girls.

"What's wrong with our one?" Carl asked Simon.

"Nothing."

"That's all you know. Deirdre broke it with her arse just now." More giggles. "But that's not the point," Carl went on, moving a little closer to Simon. "This is— what are you doing with this posh little cow?"

Emily bristled. She swore at him.

"Charming," one of the brothers said.

"Filthy," Katie Fern agreed.

"Ooh, *dear*," Carl said. "You watch your language when you're with our Simon, love. He's a good little boy."

"Get lost." Emily picked up her sled cord and turned, but Carl stretched out a great thick arm and blocked her way. "Hold on," he said. "I want to see what's so good about this thing." He wrenched the cord from Emily's hands and sat heavily down on the sled. There was an audible crack. The two girls shrieked with glee.

A thin bolt of anger pierced Emily like an electric charge. Almost before she knew what she was doing, she had leaped across and kicked Carl Allen on the shin as hard as she could. He roared with pain and fell back, clutching his leg.

One of the other brothers stepped forward and lashed out at her with a fist. In a daze she felt herself land heavily in the snow. The boy loomed over her; he lifted back a boot—Oh God, he was going to kick her!—then she saw Simon fling himself on his brother from the side and carry him facedown beside the sled.

Emily struggled to her feet. Simon and his brother were wrestling to and fro, Simon just landing a punch; Carl Allen was still holding his shin in agony, the other brother was coming forward—and suddenly Katie Fern was bearing down on her, both fists flailing.

In an instant they were grappling and Emily was having her hair pulled and pulling in return; in pain and desperation she stuck her foot behind Katie's ankle and pushed savagely. Katie toppled with a squawk and fell flat on her back.

Emily looked across. Simon was on his feet again, fending off two brothers, but his time was almost up. With ponderous intent Carl rose, pushed his brothers aside and, reaching Simon, walloped him hard. Simon fell down. Carl raised his fist again. At that moment an unexpected thing happened.

Out of nowhere a speeding missile appeared. It collided with Carl. The missile was in the form of a rather gangly figure, who wrapped his arms around Carl's neck and twisted him backward so forcefully that he lost his balance and crashed to the ground. Carl cried out and clutched at his neck. Marcus sat up beside him, looking about in a dazed sort of way.

"Well done, Marcus!" Emily shouted, then—"Watch out!"

Carl Allen clouted Marcus hard across the face. Marcus collapsed in the snow. Carl got to his feet, kicked him once, then, gingerly fingering his neck, turned and began to limp away along the bottom of the moat.

His retreat was the signal for the end of the fight. The others followed in their leader's wake, Katie Fern giving Emily an evil glare as she did so. Deirdre Pollard, who had spent the battle as a shrill spectator, brought up the rear.

"Giving up?" Simon called after them breathlessly.

A brother looked back. "We'll see you at home."

One by one they disappeared around the corner of the moat. Their scuffles and coughs faded on the air. Three people were left on the field of battle, tending to their wounds.

2

Simon Allen got slowly to his feet, rubbing at his jaw. He looked at Emily. "Are you okay?"

"Yeah." It felt as if most of her hair had been torn out by the roots. "Fine." She took a deep breath. "Thanks for helping me out."

"Whatever. You got Katie, I saw."

"Yeah."

"Good. She's a silly cow. And Carl'll feel his leg for a while. That's good too."

There was a plaintive groan beside them. Marcus was still sitting in the snow. He was bleeding a little from one nostril.

Simon crouched down beside him. "Are you all right?"

"Mnngh."

"I'm sorry. . . . My brother—that was good though, when you piled in. He didn't know what hit him."

Marcus rose onto one elbow and rubbed the side of his face. "Nor did I," he said in a bunged-up voice.

"Sorry." Simon looked up at Emily. "That was great though, eh? Gave Carl something to think about."

"He dropped this." Emily held up a small brass flask with a clear panel on the flank. Yellowy liquid sloshed about inside.

"Oh, that's mine." Marcus held out a hand. "I could do with that now." He took the flask from her, unscrewed the top, and took a short swig. Then he held it out again. "Have some."

"What is it?" Simon asked.

"Whisky, what d'you think?"

"I don't—" Emily began, but Simon had taken the flask. When he had drunk, he coughed briefly and held it out to her. She paused.

"Go on," said Marcus. "It won't kill you."

Emily took the flask and raised it to her lips. The whisky stung her mouth, filling it with burning heat and a strong peaty taste. She swallowed hastily, shuddered, and made a rasping noise. Simon grinned.

"Don't you like it? It is a bit strong."

"Top quality that," said Marcus. "Bell's. It'll help clear my nose out."

He took another gulp and returned the flask to his pocket.

"Where did you get that?" Simon said. "You didn't buy it."

Marcus shrugged. "My dad."

"Won't he skin you?"

"He won't notice."

Emily rubbed the last tears from her eyes. "You'd better get up out of the snow," she said. "You're soaking."

Marcus stood and began to brush vigorously at the snow carpeting his front. Emily looked at her watch.

"I should go," she said.

"I was going to have a look inside the keep," Marcus said. "Why don't you two come along?"

"You can't," Emily said. "It's closed. It doesn't open in the winter."

"What, you can't get in?"

"Nope. All locked up."

"Wow, that's great," he said unexpectedly. "You mean, the keep's intact?"

"Nah," Simon said. "It's ruined. No one lives there."

"It's got all four walls, if that's what you mean," Emily replied.

"The roof's fallen in," Simon went on. "It's a dump. Full of birds' nests."

Marcus did not seem put off. "There's a castle near

where I live," he said. "I used to go all the time to read and stuff. It's on a mound, and there are bits of wall with a couple of windows and a good view from the top. I loved that castle when I was a kid. I thought it was the best, thought I was king. Not anymore. There's not enough of it left—you can't imagine anything properly." He dabbed at his nose with a tissue. "But *this* place," he went on, "this is the real thing. You must come here all the time."

"Nope," Emily said.

"Three pounds fifty," Simon said.

Marcus frowned. "What?"

"Three pounds fifty. That's what it costs to get in. When it's open. Three pounds fifty for a few stone walls and bird shit on your shoes. We're not queuing up exactly."

"I've been once," Emily said, laughing. "Before we moved here. It was all right."

"All right?" Marcus cried. He seemed almost angry. "You don't know how lucky you are! I'd be here every day."

Simon shrugged. "You'd be on your own. So—" This was to Emily. "You heading off?"

"I guess so."

He nudged her sled with the toe of his boot. "I don't reckon Carl's bust it badly. We could sled a bit if you want. I'm in no hurry to go home."

Emily hesitated. She still half remembered the first attack, with Simon part of the taunting crowd. Then she thought about yet another long afternoon sitting silently beside her parents, watching television and eating nuts that made her throat itch, and she was grateful for his offer.

"Go on, then," she said. "What about you, Marcus?"

Marcus had moved a little way off, scuffing snow between his shoes. His brows were furrowed; he did not look at them. "No," he said. "I told you. I'm going to look round the keep." Without another word, he stumped off along the moat, his hands shoved deep in his pockets, his head down, thin shoulders high.

Simon watched him go. "He's weird, I reckon," he said.

"He's okay. Helped you out."

"Yeah, I guess."

Rather against Emily's expectations, sledding with Simon was good fun. To get extra speed, they took turns pushing the sled on a long run up to the edge. Simon could push so fast that Emily felt herself take off as she shot over the brink. He was also much more agile than he looked and could pull the sled back up the slope without any trouble.

After half an hour, the snow on the slope below the wall was sliced to ribbons. They came to a halt and looked up at the darkening sky. Glowering clouds hung heavily over Castle Field, and a first few lazy flakes were falling.

"Snow's up," Simon said. "Shall we pack it in?"

"Yes. I'm freezing."

Together, they set off along the bottom of the moat toward the steps that led up to the bridge. They trudged in a silence that quickly became awkward. Emily searched for something to say.

"Thanks for bringing me my hat," she said at last.

Simon grunted. "'S all right." Silence again.

"You didn't have to."

Silence. Emily ran out of inspiration. They walked a little farther.

She tried again. "So, you've got four brothers, then?"

Another grunt. "Yeah. And my sister, Pauline."

"You're the youngest, right?"

"Yeah. Mart's the eldest, twenty-three."

"He's the one—" Emily broke off almost as she began.

"He's the one inside, if that's what you mean." His voice was toneless, carefully neutral. He probably didn't like to talk about it. She certainly wouldn't if she were him.

"I'd like to have brothers," she said.

Simon flicked a look at her, perhaps gauging whether she was being ironic. "You reckon?" he said. "You saw what they're like. Beat me up the whole time, me being the youngest. I wish *I* had a younger brother. Then I could beat someone else up for a change."

"What about your sister?"

"Her? She's the worst of the lot! A bloody cat, she is. You not got brothers, then?"

"Nope. Nor sisters. Just me, Mum, and Dad."

Simon nodded. "Can't imagine that. Must be quiet."

"Very."

They were almost at the steps when the gray sky suddenly and silently unleashed its burden. Small grit-size flakes fell, first sporadically, then in greater force, and the light around them drained away. A bitter wind whipped the snow up into their faces, stinging their skin.

"Where did this come from?" Emily said. "I can't see a thing."

"Make for the gatehouse," Simon shouted. Emily could barely hear him. The squall was buffeting her parka hood against her ears. She led the way up the steps, her feet searching out the planks that formed each raise. To her left, the moat ditch was an insubstantial well of gray and white.

At the twenty-first step, the gray stones of the gatehouse wall appeared alongside; at the twenty-fourth, Emily arrived on the wooden bridge that the heritage company had constructed across the moat. Its squared yellowed timbers were hidden under several inches of snow. The ruined arch of the gatehouse was on her right, and she passed quickly into the shadow of its protection. Beyond, through the billowing curtain of snow, she glimpsed the looming mass of the castle keep.

Simon's lips were blue with cold. "Come on," he said. "The gatehouse room will be better than this."

He went through the arch and ducked around to the right. Four icebound steps led down to a low doorway in the gatehouse wall. Simon disappeared into the darkness and immediately gave a loud yell.

"What is it?" Emily was close behind him, heart thudding.

"Nothing." Simon's voice was disgusted. "Just this idiot. Startled me, that's all."

Emily came alongside, her eyes adjusting to the semidarkness. "Marcus!"

"Fancy seeing you here."

Marcus gave them a cheery grin. He was standing in a corner of the gatehouse chamber. It was a small, damp, evil-smelling room, lit only by the half-light issuing through the doorway and the arrow slit in the opposite wall. There was a low ledge to sit on. The floor was made of broken flagstones, scattered with stones and litter.

Marcus was rubbing his hands. His moodiness seemed to have vanished. "Great storm," he said. "Had a good sled?"

"Yes. How was the keep? Locked?"

"Like you said. But listen, I found something interesting. I'm glad to see you—I wanted—"

"Someone's had a cigarette in here," Simon said abruptly.

"That's not all they've had," Emily said, wrinkling her nose. A thought struck her. "You don't think there's a guard around, do you?"

Marcus grinned. "Not for about four hundred years."

"You know what I mean. There might be security."

"Not in this weather," Simon said. "He'll be at home."

"*Is* there someone?" Emily asked. "A guard?"

"There's a caretaker. Harris. You must've seen him about. Red-faced bloke. Lives in that house in the woods. We used to hide in the bushes and pelt him with stuff when he was in his garden. Drove him out of his mind. Bad-tempered sod, he is and all."

"I'd be bad tempered if you'd been chucking things at me," Marcus said.

"Oh, it was only cones and chestnuts and stuff. But one time he caught Carl skulking out the back. He was livid. He dragged him into his garden, and you know those long garden canes? Well, he ripped one out of the ground, bent Carl arse-up over his fence and gave him a real beating."

"Blimey." Emily was impressed. "He did that to Carl? He must be Goliath."

"Nah, this was years back. Carl wasn't so big then. Anyway, our dad went over that night and gave Harris a thrashing. He didn't call the police or anything, so that was that. But he's a nasty old sod, anyway."

"Wouldn't want him to find us here, then," Emily said.

"Don't worry, he's at home by the fire."

"Wish I was," said Emily. She sat down on the ledge. Simon sat beside her.

"I'm in no hurry getting back," Simon said gloomily. "Carl and Neil will be waiting for me." He sighed.

"What *is* their problem?" Emily said savagely.

Simon didn't answer. He kicked his legs back and forth against the wall. Marcus had left the conversation and was standing on the ledge, squinting out of the arrow slit. The wind whistled against the stones. A few flakes spilled in through the hole.

Simon cursed suddenly. "I'm sick of it!" he said. "Sick of being pushed around. Even Pauline does it, though she's only a year older. And a *girl*."

"Cheers," Emily said.

"You know what I mean. Ah, what's the point?" He relapsed into surly silence.

"Maybe you don't have to stick it," Marcus said. "Forget them. Rebel a bit. Do something different for a change."

"Something different? There's nothing different *to* do. You've seen the village. What's it got? A post office. A grocer's—open half days only. A pub I can't go to . . . That's it! Oh, and a garage half a mile up the road. Then nothing except fields and fens till you get to King's Lynn, and there's bugger all there, either."

"It's the same for me," said Emily.

"I suppose you like it."

"You reckon? I'm bored out of my mind."

"How can you be bored in here?" Marcus came away from the arrow slit. He seemed to have forgotten the cold. "Look around you! This place is great."

"No, it isn't," Emily said. "It's freezing, there's no light, and it smells—"

"Yeah, but that's just the surface." Marcus sat down

beside them. "I mean *apart* from that. I wish we could wait here until dark. Then we might see something."

"Like what?"

"Ghosts, maybe."

"Yeah, right."

"Well, think about it . . ." Marcus's voice fell to a conspiratorial whisper. Without quite meaning to, Emily and Simon leaned forward to catch his words. "This guardroom is *bound* to be haunted. Think of all the battles fought just beyond this wall. All the sieges. There must have been dozens. The archers in here would have been the best in the guard. They'd have killed hundreds of men . . . firing until the moat was choked with bodies. But some of the archers would have died here too, shot in the heart with arrows through this very window, or cut down when the enemy burst in at the door. It *must* have happened. I can feel it."

Emily looked about her. The room was filled with shadow.

"After all that," Marcus went on, "there's bound to be at least one lonely spirit who comes back, to moan over the place where he met his end and perhaps seek revenge on the living."

"I don't believe in ghosts," Emily said, shoving her hands firmly into her pockets.

"I do," Marcus said.

"How come?"

"Seen one."

Emily snorted. "You are such a liar."

"Don't believe me if you don't want to. Anyway"—
Marcus pushed himself off the ledge and dropped to the
flagstones—"that's not the only reason to get excited
round here. I want to show you something, up at the
keep."

Emily swung her foot at him. "Don't try to change
the subject! You can't think of something fast enough,
can you? I knew you hadn't seen one."

Marcus shrugged. "I'll tell you someday if I feel like
it. But listen, before the storm blew up I was coming
back to show you what I noticed at the keep. I can't
believe you haven't seen it yourselves."

"What?"

"Come with me and I'll show you."

Simon groaned. "Just tell us about it," he snapped.
"It's a blizzard out there."

"The snow's dying off. Come on, it'll only take a
minute."

Emily went to the doorway and looked out. Sure
enough, only a few tattered flakes of snow were drifting
haphazardly around in the air. The wind had slackened.

"It's breaking," she said, looking at her watch. "Look,

I've really got to get home. Can you show me quickly, on the way back?"

"'Course. Come on—" Marcus nudged Simon, who was evidently still reluctant. "It'll be worth it. It'll make you forget your stupid brothers."

"And Pauline," Emily said.

"All right." Simon heaved himself to his feet. "I owe you both one for earlier. But it had better be good."

Marcus led them outside and up the steps. The light was better now and there was a clear view all around. For a moment Marcus halted.

"Get on with it, then," Simon said.

"Yeah, in a minute." Marcus was standing spellbound, gazing straight ahead.

The great square keep rose up whole and strong to the height of a four-story building. It sat in the middle of its flat, white enclosure, surrounded by the raised mound of the moat's inner edge and here and there by low broken stretches of the curtain wall. It was built of gray stones, with a squared tower at each corner. Except at the base, where they sloped steeply outward, the walls were sheer and blank. In their lower halves there were no openings except for arrow slits, but higher up, near where the wall began to fracture into ruin, several small arched windows could be glimpsed, separated by ornate columns.

"Wouldn't you just love to get in there?" Marcus said.

"Sure," Emily said. "Except that it's locked."

"Like we keep saying," Simon added.

"Follow me." Marcus set off across the snow, making for the left-hand corner of the keep. "What's it like inside?" he asked.

"Um, it's okay," Emily said. "Good for kids. Stairs and passages and stuff."

"Is there a dungeon?"

"Um . . . I don't remember. Haven't been in it for years."

"What about that tower? Can you get up it? It looks complete."

"I think so. Come back in the spring—you'll be able to climb it then."

"Three pounds fifty," Simon reminded him. "Get your mum and dad to take you."

"I can do better than that."

They passed the corner of the left-hand tower. Just beyond was a rounded stone arch with a narrow rim and stone columns in the wall on either side. In the arch was a great wooden double door, studded with black nails. A large keyhole was set in the left-hand door at chest height. Marcus looked through the hole, but could see nothing.

"There's stairs there," Emily said. "It's roofed, that's why it's dark."

Marcus pushed at the door, but the massive rough wood did not budge. He stood back and looked up. "Norman," he said. "You can tell by the round arch. Must be quite early."

"Is this it?" Simon asked.

"No. Come on." Marcus moved off along the side of the keep. "Once you got in there you could hold out for months. You'd barricade the door, maybe put a portcullis behind it so they couldn't smash it down. Then you'd sit back. No one would have a hope in hell of getting past these walls." He craned his neck to look up at the mass of stone stretching into the white sky.

"The army wouldn't have to break them down," Emily said. "They'd just starve you out."

Marcus shook his head. "You'd have tons of food with you before you started. There'll be great store-houses in there, deep in the foundations, where you could put your oats or whatever. Nice and dark and cool, so they wouldn't go off. And you'd have a con-stant supply of fresh water."

"What, from a stream?" Simon asked.

"No, a well. There'll be one in the cellars, cut through the rock to a water source. It'll never dry up. Now, past this corner . . ."

They rounded the second tower, and a new side of the keep stretched before them. Three-quarters of the way along, Marcus stopped and pointed. Emily and Simon looked up at the wall. The stonework here had evidently once been subjected to some intense bombardment. Its top was ragged, much lower than most other parts of the keep. In one place, there was a great vertical gash that ran halfway down the wall. It passed in a zigzag fashion through several ruined windows and ended in a roundish hole only five meters or so above the ground.

"See that hole? That's not so high up," Marcus said in a thoughtful voice.

"What's the big deal?" Simon said.

"Look inside it," Marcus went on. "See the two metal bars running across the hole? I reckon there's a walkway or something behind it at that level. Is there, Em? You've been in—you must remember."

Emily frowned. "Yeah, maybe . . ." she said doubtfully. "You can walk round the inside of the keep on some sort of ledge. Why? Does it matter?"

Marcus's eyes were bright with excitement. He grinned. "Depends whether you want to get inside or not! Check out the base of the wall."

They checked it out. For nearly all their height, the massive walls of the keep were vertical. But about three meters from the ground, the walls suddenly jutted out diagonally, spearing down at an angle into the snow. This meant the base of the walls formed a very steep— and icy—ramp.

"They did that to strengthen the structure," Marcus said, "in case the enemy tried to tunnel under to make the walls collapse. But the thing is that if you were careful you could shin up that sloping bit. Then you'd be halfway to the hole. Simon might even be able to reach it from there if he stretched. Anyway, if you then climbed the wall, which wouldn't be too hard, you'd be laughing—you could just squeeze through the hole into the passage!" He paused triumphantly.

"There's a few big ifs in there," Simon said.

"We couldn't get up," Emily said flatly. "It's too high. Nice idea, anyway."

"You see what I mean, though?" Marcus said to Simon. "Half of it's on the slope." Without warning, he suddenly ran as fast as he could at the sloping masonry at the foot of the wall, leaping up it in two, three steps. On the third step his trainers slipped and he crashed forward against the snowy stone, then very gently slid back down the slope to the bottom.

"Well done," said Emily.

Marcus ignored her. "It's slippery, obviously," he said, getting to his feet, "but we could scrape the ice off easily enough. Then we could scramble to the top of the base and be near the hole."

"Not that near," Simon said. "We couldn't stretch to it, and even if we could, *most* of us couldn't pull ourselves up." His emphasis suggested that "most" meant two thirds.

"Couldn't we climb the wall, though?"

Emily looked at her watch. She didn't have time for Marcus's mad enthusiasms. But she was uneasy to see that Simon, far from brushing off the harebrained scheme, was entering into the spirit of the idea. Something in the practical nature of the challenge seemed to appeal to him. He had approached the foot of the masonry spur and was looking up at the stonework beyond.

"It's quite rough," he said. "Those stones there are smooth, but these other ones have been worn back quite a way. I reckon I might get a foothold. Could I climb up? Maybe. Don't know how far."

"The worn stones go right up to the hole," Marcus pointed out. "You could do it, Simon. And if you got in, you could help us up too."

Emily thought it was time to intervene. "Yeah, go for it," she said. "If you want to break your neck."

"It's not that difficult," Marcus said. "Come on, Simon, we've got to try!"

"I'm going," Emily said. "I don't want any falling idiots landing on me."

Simon said nothing. He just stood there, considering the wall. Emily loitered. Marcus hopped about in a fit of impatience. At last, after a full minute of silence, Simon finally spoke.

"No," he said. "I reckon Em's right. *I* might be able to do it, but you'd both fall off and break something."

"But—" Marcus began.

"It's a stupid idea," Simon said. "Who wants to get in the castle, anyway? What would we do there? Come on, let's go."

Marcus muttered something under his breath and turned away from the wall. In gloomy silence, they set off back the way they had come. Emily was first. She rounded the corner of the tower and walked into a man standing there. She screamed. The man shot out an arm and grabbed her by the hood of her parka. Emily tried to pull away, but the man jerked her toward him so forcefully that the fabric of her hood ripped. Behind her, Simon and Marcus were transfixed.

"You're not going anywhere!" the man said, shaking Emily hard by the hood. "What do you think you're doing? Eh? Eh?" With each exclamation he gave her another shake, making her whimper with terror. Emily was so frightened she could barely focus: all she could see was a white-haired, scarlet-faced apparition scowling at her in fury.

"Let her go," Simon said in a shaky voice. "You don't need to do that."

The man's gaze fell on Simon. "I know you," he said. "Trespassing again? You ought to be locked up with the rest of your family."

Simon went white. He said nothing.

His hand still clawing in Emily's hood, the man gestured for them to start walking in the direction of the gatehouse.

"Come on, get going!" he shouted. "Every bloody winter it's the same. You vandals think you can waltz in here, damaging the stones, churning up the grass, leaving litter everywhere like it's a bloody garbage dump. . . . No you don't, my son, come here!" This was to Marcus, who was wandering off stealthily at a slight angle to the caretaker's intended route. A quick step to the side, a clip to the head, and Marcus was back on line, rubbing his scalp in shock.

"Didn't expect that, did you?" the caretaker said shortly, dropping back so that all three were well in front of him. "That's what naughty boys get if they go trespassing. And if they still don't heed, we'll see what the police have to say about it. Understand?" He gave Emily's hood a corresponding yank.

"We weren't doing any harm," Simon said. Of all of them, he seemed the one least stunned by their capture. Marcus and Emily were both unable to speak. "Don't get the police over, please," he went on in a plaintive tone. "We won't do it again."

"I should think you won't, my lad. Because I'll be looking out for you. I'm here every day, see? And rain or snow, I'll collar you if you set so much as one foot in these grounds. What was it—through the hedge?" He tugged at Emily again. "Well? Speak up! You came in through the hedge somewhere, did you? Eh?"

Emily nodded dumbly.

"Every year it's the same. How old do you think that hedge is? No, you haven't given it a moment's thought, have you? Two hundred years old that hedge is, and you're happy to slash holes in it just so you can get in to play in the snow! You're bloody thoughtless kids, and if I had my way they'd lock you up to teach you a few hard lessons. Right, through here—" They had reached the gatehouse. "—now head for the entrance gate. Yes, you don't know where that is, do you, miss? Not used to paying your way, eh? Keep going. . . ."

A constant stream of commentary like this accompanied them as they walked in dismal fashion down to the gate, a revolving metal grille set in the hedge next to a tiny wooden cabin. The caretaker stood by while they passed hurriedly through the grille, hearing it click back into position behind each one.

"Right," he said, staring at them through the narrow bars. "You've been let off lightly this time. Now, clear off. I've told you what I'll do if I see you here again—"

But the three were already walking away from him as fast as they could, down the road alongside the frosted hedge. The road was thick with compressed ice, and after a couple of steps, Emily slipped, lost her footing, and fell, landing hard on one elbow. There was a loud laugh from the caretaker at the gate. Silently, Simon and Marcus helped her to her feet. They walked on.

At last Simon risked a look behind them. "He's gone," he said, stopping in the road. "That bastard."

"That tosser," Marcus said.

"What a git the man is."

"Treating us like bloody hooligans, like kids."

"If I was bigger I'd give him something."

"Like stupid—like vandalizing kids."

"He'd know about it and all."

"That *tosser.*"

Simon looked at Marcus. "You haven't got any more of that whisky, have you?" he asked.

"Finished it."

"Oh."

Emily said nothing. The shock of the encounter was still sinking in. She sniffed.

"Hey, don't worry about him, Em," Simon said. "He's all mouth."

"Yeah." She said it in a small voice.

"Are you worried he'll tell your dad?"

She frowned. "No!" It came out more violently than she'd meant it to. "It's not that. It was just . . . he was just so horrible."

"Forget about him. He's nothing."

"Yeah, but he wins, doesn't he? We all stood there and took it." Her fear changed and hardened into anger. "We all lined up meekly and trotted out in front of him like good little children. And that's it. He wins. Like your brother. He beat us up and won too."

"Carl didn't win! Marcus here made him look a complete pillock in front of those girls."

"At the cost of my nose," Marcus said.

"It didn't *feel* like a victory," Emily said. "Anyway, we're turfed out and there's not much we can do about it, is there?" She scuffed her boot against the snowy bank on the verge of the road.

"Carl didn't win," Simon muttered.

"Well, I think we should do something," Marcus said.

"Like what?" Simon looked up. "I'd only get duffed

up again. I've booked myself one kicking for tonight already."

"I'm not talking about Carl. The *castle*. That tossing caretaker. So what if he won this time? You're being too defeatist, Em. It's no shame to be beaten back by the enemy. In every siege it was the same. The defenders would charge out in a surprise attack, send the besieging forces packing, kill a few—then, when they couldn't break up the surrounding circle, they had to nip back inside the castle and hole up as before. Then the besiegers would settle in again. It was a game of patience."

"What, a card game?" Emily grinned weakly, despite herself.

Marcus gave a cry of annoyance. "You know! A waiting game is what I mean. It's the same with us."

"So we go in again, and sooner or later he'll find us and boot us out again! What's the point?"

"He won't find us—" Marcus said, "—if we're inside the castle."

There was a silence.

"But we've already said—" Emily began.

"I know what we said. But that was before. And Simon knows we could do it."

Emily looked at Simon. He said nothing.

"Think about it. We'd be inside, watching him

plodding about, looking for us in the snow. He'd never bother with the castle. Think how sweet that would be."

Emily thought. It did seem sweet.

"I reckon I *could* get in," Simon said. "And if I had a rope, maybe you could too. I could get one and all. My dad's got some in the shed."

"Brilliant!" Marcus clapped his hands together. "That's settled, then! We'll restore our honor. Tomorrow?"

After a long moment, Simon nodded. "Okay," he said slowly. "If Em's on for it."

They looked at her. Emily remembered the livid face, the repeated tugs on her hood. Her neck was sore.

"I'm on for it," she said.

Marcus grinned. "So what time?"

"It'll have to be after lunch," said Emily. "Two. I've got aunts visiting till then. What about you, Simon?"

"Two's okay. If I'm still alive." He scratched his chin ruefully.

"Marcus?"

"Any time's good for me."

"Don't your parents ever want you for anything?"

"No. Well, my bike's back this way. I'll see you here at two. Happy aunting. Happy kicking." Abruptly he turned and set off back up the road, following the hedge. Emily and Simon watched him go.

"He *is* weird, you know," Simon said.

"My bike's that way too," Emily said at last. "Will you be okay?"

"Oh, yeah, I'll be fine."

"Tomorrow . . ."

"We'll give it a shot. If it's difficult, we'll give it up. Whatever Marcus says."

"See you tomorrow, then."

"Yeah."

Simon walked off slowly down the road. Emily ran in the opposite direction. She was very late.

CAPTURE

3

At half past two, Emily arrived at the lane, flustered after a prolonged lunch and an endless good-bye. She was hot, bothered, and late. As she came out of the trees under the gray slab of the sky, she saw Simon and Marcus waiting for her near where they had parted the day before. They were standing together awkwardly in silence, Simon hefting a large rucksack over one shoulder, Marcus smoking a cigarette. Marcus was coughing as she approached, looking ill and white in the face, but as he caught Emily's disapproving eye, he took another short drag. The end flared red, then died.

"Thought I'd try one out," he said defiantly.

"Go right ahead," Emily said. "If you want to kill yourself."

"I will." There was a pause. Emily looked at Simon. He nodded at her in greeting.

"You've never had one, I suppose," Marcus said.

"No."

"What, not ever?"

"No."

"I don't believe you. You must have tried. Ah, you're blushing."

"No, I'm not. Shut up about it."

"I've got the rope," Simon said.

"Well, I bet *he* has," Marcus went on. "Haven't you?"

Simon ignored him. "Nicked it from my dad's shed. Used to use it with his trailer. I reckon it's long enough."

He opened the loose top of the rucksack and held it open for Emily to look inside. It was filled with coarse, brown rope.

"It's like the ones at school," Emily said.

"Yeah, but thinner. Can you climb them to the top?"

"Mostly."

"What about you?" Simon proffered the open rucksack to Marcus. "Could you climb that? No point us going if you can't."

Marcus's cigarette was burning down to a stump. He threw it onto the snow and trod on it. "Of course. Wouldn't have suggested it otherwise, would I? We'd better get on with it. It'll be dark in a couple of hours."

"Has anyone seen him? Harris, I mean." Emily

looked over at the thick shadows of the hedge beside them.

"I know who you mean." Simon was irritable. Evidently he shared her nerves. "No, but we're not through the hedge yet. We'll have to go carefully."

"Where are we getting in?"

"Farther along. Where the hedge is closest to the moat. Less far to run."

Simon tightened the drawstrings on his rucksack and slung it over his shoulder. Then the three of them set off along the hedge. When they got to the entrance gate, they slipped one by one across its mouth, keeping low, scanning the snow beyond the grille for any sign of movement. Everything was quiet. They continued along the hedge, circling out a little way to avoid treading in the deepest drifts. Already Emily could feel her heart pounding, and as yet she wasn't even breaking the law. She followed close on Simon's heels, with Marcus scuffling and slipping behind her. Several times she heard him cough messily under his breath. He was in an odd mood. Perhaps he was nervous too.

They crossed the car park and made a small diversion over a gate into the next field, which undulated with frozen furrows. The castle hedge continued on their right, and Simon kept as close as possible to it. At last they came to a spot where the hedge was thin and scrappy. Simon shrugged the rucksack off his back and knelt in the snow, peering through the patchwork of holes between the branches. The others flopped down beside him.

"Can't see anything," Simon whispered. "We're not spotted yet—and if you stop doing that it might stay that way." This was to Marcus, who was coughing again into his hand.

"Just a tickle in my throat."

"Serves you right," Emily said.

"Yeah, yeah."

"Okay." Simon grabbed the rucksack and began pushing it through the gap in front of them. "I'm going first. I'll peg it to the edge of the moat. If all's clear, I'll wave for you, Emily, to follow. Then Marcus. Okay?"

He shoved the rucksack across and began to wriggle after it, plowing through the snow and cursing softly whenever a root or bramble snared him. In thirty seconds he had got to his feet, and with a quick look in all directions, was off over Castle Field, bending almost double as he ran. Emily and Marcus watched him go.

"He's enjoying this, isn't he?" Marcus said.

"He's there!"

Simon turned and signaled briefly. Immediately, Emily began squeezing through the gap on her stomach, ignoring the chill that permeated her clothing.

Then she was out and up and running through the snow, fearful all the while of hearing the caretaker's hideous voice, seeing him erupting from some hiding place in the ground.

"All clear so far," Simon said, as Emily half fell to a halt beside him on the lip of the moat. He turned to signal Marcus. Emily looked around and saw that Simon had chosen their route well. They were on the correct side of the keep: she could see the great tear ripping down through the stonework to the hole. It looked horribly high up. She shook her head at the stupidity of their plan.

Marcus appeared beside them, wheezing gently. No sooner had he sunk down than Simon gestured at the moat. "It's steep," he said. "But we should cross it here. If we go round trying to find an easy bit, we might expose ourselves."

Skidding down was easy enough, but the opposite ascent was hard. They had to yank themselves up a little at a time, forcing their numb fingers under the snow to grip on to the crispy grass beneath. When they got to the top, they were only fifty meters from the keep walls. Still there was no sign of anyone.

Simon grinned. "Come on, then," he said.

All three ran the last leg, arriving at the wall together.

"Good job it's not snowed," Marcus said. "Our tracks

will mingle with yesterday's. Won't be spotted. Well—off you go, then, Simon."

"Wait till I get my breath back. And I need to plan my route and all."

Simon unpacked the rope with difficulty, spilling it to the ground in a tangle of heavy coils. He searched for an end and pulled one out at last. It had a piece of thick cord tied securely to it. Simon looped this cord several times around the back of his belt and fixed it with a complicated knot. Marcus and Emily watched, agog.

"Won't it be too heavy for you to lift?" Emily asked.

"Should be okay as long as you spool the rope out so that I don't get the full weight of it, or it knots or anything. One of you's got to do that. The other keeps lookout. If there's any sign of Harris or anyone else, let me know right off or we'll all be stuffed."

Marcus volunteered to hold the rope, and Simon readied himself for the climb. Checking that the rope was loose and free behind him, he set his hands high and wide apart on the icy buttress wall. His fingers dug in between the stones and found their grip. Then he kicked first one boot, then another at the wall below, chipping off wedges of ice so that each toe cap could rest in a small depression. When both boots were secure, he stretched up higher and dug in his fingers again. In this way, slowly, hesitantly, and with several slips of both boots, he began to move up the buttress wall with the rope hanging down behind him.

"Well done, Simon!" Emily said. She said it in a loud whisper, conscious of every sound. As she spoke, she walked past the near tower and cautiously peered around it at the next face of the keep. All along that side the way was clear.

"The trouble comes if Harris rounds that far corner," she said to Marcus, who was standing at the base of the buttress, feeding out the rope. "He'll recognize us a mile off."

"He won't," Marcus said. "Turn up, I mean. Anyway, if he did, I'd just run. He might know where you two live, but he'd not have a clue about me."

"Cheers. That's good to know. Hey, look—he's made it!"

Sure enough, Simon had scaled the buttress wall almost to its top. Now he was sprawled upon it, his boots wedged into a foothold while his hands sought a good grip on the first vertical blocks of stone. There were two blocks that had been severely weathered around the edges. Simon grasped these, and with a swift heave, pulled himself higher. A few quick adjustments, a scrabble of the arms, and in a moment he was standing upright, fingers hooked into the wall, feet resting at the very top of the buttress.

"Nice one!" Marcus whispered. "You're almost there!"

It seemed that for Simon, the difficult part was over. Now that he had reached the bumpy part of the wall, his progress was much quicker and more confident. They watched him clamber up, ever nearer to the hole.

Marcus spooled out the rope. "He's good at this," he said lightly. "Did you say his brother was in prison for something? Was it burglary, by any chance?"

Emily frowned at him. "Shut up, Marcus. It was your stupid idea in the first place—that's why he's doing it."

"Yes, I'm just saying he's got a natural gift for it, that's all."

"What's wrong with you today? Shut up!" Emily turned full circle, scanning the horizon. Then she walked to the edge of the tower and peered around it again. No one was in sight. A soft cheer sounded behind her. Marcus was waving his arms and pointing.

"He's done it!" he said in a hoarse whisper. "He's got inside!" Emily looked up just in time to see Simon's boots disappearing in through the hole in the castle wall. She ran back to stand with Marcus, watching the hole. There was a pause. The rope had stopped spooling from Marcus's hands. At the point where it vanished into the hole, it twitched once or twice, but was otherwise still. Emily and Marcus stood together, eyes fixed on the hole. Nothing happened.

Terrifying possibilities ran through Emily's mind. She darted a panicky look at Marcus. "What's up?" she hissed. "Do you think maybe Harris . . . ?"

Marcus frowned, shook his head. "Nah, we'd have heard something. He's all right. Can't have fallen either, or the rope would have gone through." He didn't look too confident.

Suddenly the rope jerked in his hand, making them both start. Simon's head appeared in the hole, wearing a broad grin. He raised a cheery thumb.

"Piece of piss!" he called. "You should see it up here! It's great! Hold on a sec while I get the rope fixed." His face retreated.

"What a star!" Emily said.

Marcus shrugged, muttering something that Emily did not catch.

After a few moments, Simon reappeared above them. "Okay," he said. "The rope's tied to the railing. One of you come up."

Marcus looked at Emily. "So," he said, "who's going to follow the star?"

"Oh, you can," Emily said quickly. "It was your idea, after all."

"Yeah. Okay." He said it grudgingly, but Emily saw his face brighten.

Somewhat gingerly, Marcus approached the edge of the buttress, gathered the rope in both hands and, with his feet bolstered against the base of the wall, began to hoist himself up. He went very slowly, taking a great deal of time between each new grip and swinging side to side in an exaggerated fashion. His feet scrabbled for purchase on the buttress.

Simon was watching from above. "Come on!" he called softly. "Rest your weight properly on the wall. Plant your feet square. It's easy!"

Marcus did not reply. Emily was alarmed to see that his face had gone bright pink with the effort. He was barely at the top of the buttress and he was already struggling. Twice, one of his feet slipped against the stone and he almost lost his hold, spiraling around helplessly before managing to stabilize himself again. Emily could hear him taking great gulps of air and letting them out again too rapidly.

"Just take it steadily," she called. "You're doing fine! Isn't he, Simon?"

Simon blew his cheeks out and raised his eyes to the skies. "Yeah," he called. "Fine. Try not to let your feet get higher than your hands. The blood goes to your head."

Emily walked impatiently back and forth at the

bottom of the wall. Deciding it would be wise to stand well clear of the drop zone in case Marcus let go altogether, she idled across to the edge of the tower and glanced around it.

And went rigid with shock.

Harris was strolling along the base of the castle wall toward her. He was at the far end, next to the opposite tower, and had evidently only just turned the corner. At that moment he was irritably scanning the farthest reaches of Castle Field for signs of trespassing life. As she watched, he stopped, raised his hand over his eyes, and peered out toward the distant hedge. This was Emily's good fortune, for if he had been looking straight ahead he would certainly have seen her.

Emily jerked back out of sight, cold blood flushing through her veins.

"He's coming!" She raced back, shrieking the whisper out. To her horror, Marcus seemed to have climbed no higher than when she had last looked at him. He seemed frozen in position, unable to go either up or down.

"Harris! He's coming!"

Marcus let out a gurgle of despair, and above him, Simon banged a fist against the ragged stonework.

"Move, Marcus! You've got to speed up! Harris is coming!"

Another gurgle. "I can't . . . I'm stuck!"

"You've got to! Or we'll all be caught!"

"Oh, God . . ." Marcus's arms were shaking with the effort of holding on. He snatched his lower hand away from the rope and planted it above the other. Then he did the same with the next. It didn't seem to get him very far. His face was contorted; his feet skittered against the wall. Above him, Simon leaned out of the hole, stretching an arm down.

"That's it! A bit higher and I'll grab you! Where is he?" This was to Emily.

"By the far tower! He's stopped, but he'll be here in a minute!" She was frozen in panic, unable to decide whether to run or try to climb. The white expanse of the field offered no shelter. Perhaps the moat . . . but then she'd be leaving Marcus—and Simon—to their fate. Her eyes flicked from Marcus's dangling form to the empty space at the corner of the tower. Any moment now he might appear.

"Come *on*, Marcus!" His feet were kicking frantically at the wall, as if he wanted to run up it. She could hear Simon muttering encouragement and invective. His hand was outstretched. Marcus swayed back and forth, inching upward with every swing.

He would never make it, and even if he did she could never follow him in time. She thought of her previous attempts at rope-climbing in the school gym—the pain in the arms, the watery weakness in her muscles. She didn't have a hope.

Simon was now half out of the hole, preventing himself from falling by locking the back of his knees under the lower of the two metal rails that spanned the gap. His outstretched fingers swiped the air a little above Marcus's swaying head.

"Reach up!" he hissed through gritted teeth. "I'll pull you."

Marcus made a Herculean effort. He wedged a foot against the wall, lifted a hand, gripped, strained—and noticeably advanced up the rope. His other hand stretched out, wavered—and was seized so firmly in Simon's fist that Marcus cried out in pain. Immediately, Simon began to wriggle back through the hole, pushing himself with his free hand. As he retreated, Marcus seemed to levitate: he looked to be rising up the wall of his own free will. In a matter of seconds he was at the hole. For a moment his bottom and legs dangled in thin air, then a hand appeared, grabbing him by the back of his belt and yanking him out of sight. There was a distant yelp.

Emily was already on the rope. No sooner had Marcus disappeared than she took hold and began to climb, frantically going hand over hand, ignoring any doubts, slips of the feet, the aches in her muscles. Her eyes were locked on the stones of the wall in front of her, but she could sense the distance above and the terrible proximity of the corner of the tower. How quiet it was. No sound came from Marcus or Simon. Her boots scuffled on the stones. Her blood pounded in her ears.

Hand over hand. Step over step. The top of the buttress appeared. There was better grip on the stones here—she could push up with her feet, as if on a ladder. The muscles of her shoulders cracked; they felt like they were tearing. She tried to block out the memory of her many failures on the ropes of the gym.

In her head she could see Harris walking. He must be very close now. Stride after stride. Long legs going. Head craning forward. Eyes open. Coming nearer. A bird of prey at the corner of the tower.

He would hear her feet on the stones, hear the rope flicking against the wall. Now he would be running, arms out, ready to round the corner and seize the rope, shake her loose, and let her drop.

Hand over hand over hand.

Suddenly her hood was seized and lifted and she was drawn upward and forward into the hole with her zipper digging into her throat. Two hands grabbed her, pulled her over a jagged surface of flint, and down again onto a stone floor, where she twisted and sprawled on her back.

"Quick, quick." A whisper. An endless spool of rope descended on top of her. Four arms gave a final heave and then the end whipped past, hitting something metal with a dull impact on the way. Simon and Marcus ducked down next to her, white-faced, eyes staring.

No one breathed.

In the silence they heard footsteps crunching through snow.

The footsteps stopped.

They did not look at each other. Emily was staring at the lacerations in the toe caps of her leather boots. There were five of them on the left boot, three long, two small.

She heard Marcus give a little whimper.

The footsteps started again. Motionless, they listened to them pass away along the edge of the wall into silence.

The footsteps were gone.

Nobody moved. Nobody said anything.

4

"Well done, Emily."

She sat up, looked at Simon.

"I've never seen anyone climb so fast. You did it quicker than me."

"Sheer desperation." She was numb. Every muscle ached. "Was it you who pulled me up?"

"Yeah. Marcus took care of the rope."

"Cheers. Cheers, Marcus. So we did it, then."

"Only just. He came round from the side just as I ducked down. He might have seen the rope before we got it in, if he'd looked up."

"But he didn't."

"No." Simon slumped back against the inside of the wall. "Well done too, Marcus," he added.

Marcus was sitting opposite, wedged between them, leaning on a metal railing. He was very white, except for two red spots on his cheeks. His chest rose and fell raggedly.

"You don't have to be nice," he grunted. "I know I was crap."

"You got in," Emily said. "That's what counts."

"I'm knackered. I feel like I'm going to die."

"Give it a minute, you'll be okay."

"I feel like a cig."

"No way. That would get Harris down on us."

"How? He'd never smell it." Marcus began to fumble in the pockets of his coat.

"So go ahead and risk it. And see what happens if he comes inside."

"We *should* be careful," Simon said peaceably. "For a start, if he comes in, we're exposed up here. We need to move."

"Why should he come in? It's locked." But even so, Marcus shuffled around a little to take a look at where they were. As he did so, his hands stopped rummaging in his coat and he became silent and still.

"Oh, *yes*," he said quietly. "This is what we came for."

They were sprawled on a meter-wide stone walkway that ran along the inside of the keep wall. In most places it was roofed, but where they were lying, the ceiling had been smashed away by the same titanic impact that had forced the hole in the outer stones. Every three meters or so, an arch supported the ceiling, and across each arch, modern railings had been driven into the stonework. These provided safe support for anyone passing along the walkway.

It was a necessary precaution, for beyond the arches was a void. Far below stretched a carpeting of pristine snow.

"Floor's fallen away," Marcus said.

"Might have, don't know."

"Of course it has. See that fireplace on the same level as us?" It hung there, a carved recess opening out into nothing six meters or more above the floor. "That's a monster. That would have served the great hall, which was here on our level. We could have walked into it from this passage. But the hall floor's caved in. Down there would've been storerooms, I expect."

"Let's go and see," Simon said.

As they got to their feet, Marcus gave another exclamation. "What's that?" He pointed down through the gap at a small wooden construction sitting in the snow. "Looks like a garden shed."

Emily looked. "It's a shop. Sells guides, postcards, and stuff."

"Keep your voices down!" Simon spoke in a whisper.

"Okay, boss. Let's find some stairs." Marcus had regained his good humor. "Which way? I reckon left."

He set off, passing immediately into the relative dimness of the covered walkway. A little snow had blown in through the arches, but for the most part the flags were dark and wet. Emily smelled a peculiar cool dampness emanating from the stones, which seemed separate from the chill of the midwinter day.

"Aha!" Marcus halted. The passage ahead changed direction and continued on at ninety degrees, but here also a low arch led on to a stairwell. Steps disappeared up and down into darkness.

"Down first," Marcus said. "We need to survey our territory, gain control."

Something in his words fired them with new energy. Almost on top of one another they pelted down the steps, past a couple of arrow slits, and out through another arch into a sudden blaze of light and snow.

Into the white courtyard, open to the sky. They did not halt, but went onward, spreading out like bullets strafed from a gun, cutting trails in the clean snow of the open space. All around them gray-green walls and empty arches looked down. Conscious of the need for silence, they stilled the cries of triumph that rose in their throats, but they were seized instead with a fiercer compulsion—to run, to dance, to kick the snow in savage fountains as they went, to inscribe their presence in the forbidden place. Back and forth they ran, weaving in loops and circles, arms out like airplanes, dive-bombing each other but never touching, never catching another's eyes. Once, Simon scooped a handful of snow and tossed it toward Emily, but it was a half-hearted act, and if she noticed she did not respond.

They came to a halt separately, Marcus first, then Simon and Emily in different areas of the space. Marcus and Simon flopped down on the steps of two gaping archways. Emily propped herself against the stonework midway along a wall, raised her head, and shut her eyes.

She felt the blood throbbing in her temple, wrists, and legs. Her chest shuddered with the exertions of her heart. A wave of dizziness came, a fireworks display of white lights exploding on her retina. When it passed, she opened her eyes again.

A rim of masonry bordered the sky, jabbing its broken edges against the clouds. Weak winter light fell on the topmost stones. Two birds, either crows or ravens, passed diagonally across and disappeared behind the snipped-off columns that marked the skeleton of a window. The black sticks of their nests projected messily from several holes and sills on the wall.

Emily could hear the wind whistling through the uppermost windows, but in the belly of the keep the air was still. Her pulse was settling down; she felt warm and relaxed. Her mind drifted, fixing on a pair of narrow windows that opened inward onto a single broad internal arch. Perhaps, on a vanished level above the great hall, they had once let light into the lord's bedchamber. She could almost feel the airiness of that pleasant upper room, glimpse a far view of the woods and fields, the rushes on a stone floor, a crackling fireplace . . .

There was a low whistle. Emily came back to herself and looked around. Both Marcus and Simon had disappeared.

She waited, but when the whistle was not repeated, Emily straightened and wandered over to the shed. She brushed the frost off the single window and looked inside. Cheap guide pamphlets were stacked tidily on a shelf, along with an empty cash box and a wooden rack filled with small souvenir offerings—postcards, bookmarks, pencils, erasers. Emily remembered that she had bought one of the erasers herself, when she had visited years before. It had been a pink one with a black sketch of the keep on it, and she had been very pleased with it at the time. Now all the bits and pieces just seemed tawdry, fit only for children.

Behind the shelf were a chair, a cupboard, and what looked like some sort of heater. More in hope than expectation, Emily went around to the side of the shed and tried the door. To her vast surprise it opened. She stood rigid for a moment, her heart beating hard, then shrugged. She could hardly break in any more seriously than she had already. She stepped inside.

The floor was laid with a threadbare piece of carpet. A rack of old magazines and books was stored under the shelf, presumably to allay the boredom of the castle attendant. Otherwise, the shed was empty. Emily tried the door of the cupboard, but found it secured with a small padlock. Her attention was mostly taken up with the heater. It didn't have a cable, so it wasn't electric; if it was gas or paraffin and there was some fuel left in it, perhaps she could make it work. That would be interesting. . . .

She looked the heater over briefly, but decided not to risk trying any of the switches. Simon would probably know what to do.

Another whistle sounded as she came out. Marcus had emerged from a dark doorway beyond the hut and was signaling to her excitedly.

"I've found the well!" he called. "Where's Simon?"

"No idea. Let's see it, then."

She followed him down two shallow steps, worn into a curve at their center, out of the snow, out of the light, into a dark chamber lit only by the arch and a narrow slit in the wall. The air inside smelled wet, like a cave. Emily could see Marcus moving in the far corner of the room; she paused where she was while her eyes adjusted.

"Here it is. Look, under this grille."

His voice echoed around the chamber. He was bending down now, tugging experimentally at something. Emily came over. The floor was slippery with water.

"It's a bit loose. We might be able to pull it free."

"Don't be stupid, Marcus." She could see what he was doing now. There was a wide hole in the flagstones, a circular gap of utter blackness. On top of it was a square cover of latticed metal strips bolted to the stones at all four corners. He was tugging at one edge, which made a slight grinding noise.

"Stop pulling it. You don't want that loose. Someone could fall in."

"I wonder how deep it is. Some of these wells go hundreds of meters down into the bedrock. Let's see . . ." He turned, still crouching, and began scuffling about on the floor, feeling with his hands. "Aha—" he seized a fragment of stone and dropped it through the grille. "Listen . . ."

There was a lengthy pause. Then a dull thud sounded, far below.

"Huh." Marcus straightened. "Looks like it's dried up."

"Yeah," Emily said. "Still, leave it alone, eh?"

"Mind you, it might not be a well at all. It might be a dungeon, where they chucked enemies and left them to rot. There's a French word for it, but I've forgotten it. Yeah, that might be it. What we need's a flashlight."

"Let's go and see what Simon's doing." She knew it was irrational, but Emily found that she badly wanted to lead Marcus out of the dark room and far from the grille. Whether it was a well or a dungeon didn't matter. That hole led to a place where your bones would lie secret and forgotten, away from the world and the light.

"What are you two doing?" As they approached the bright slab that marked the entrance, Simon's form half blocked it out. "Come and see what I've found! Better than grubbing about in here."

They left the chamber and came out into the whiteness of the snowy yard.

"This way." Simon pointed along the side of the wall to another dark arch.

"What is it?" Marcus was shielding his eyes against the light.

"I'll surprise you. Do you remember it, Em?"

"Can't remember a thing. Too long ago."

Simon set off and Emily followed him, but Marcus remained rooted. "In a bit," he said. "I want to check out the hut first."

Emily looked back over her shoulder, but Marcus was already halfway to the hut. Simon paid him no attention. He went through the arch and across another dimly lit room to a spiral stairwell hidden in the corner. Up they went, their feet scraping on the stone. After a couple of rotations they passed a landing with archways leading off, but Simon continued to climb. Finally they came to another level. A passage ran to the left behind a padlocked grille; other bars blocked farther progress up the stairs. But right beside them was a door made of light wood.

"Check it out," Simon said.

Emily pushed it open and went through, down two steps into a room.

"Oh. It's lovely," she said.

It was a room of light. It was quite small and was laid with a simple wooden floor of creamy brown planking that she knew immediately must be modern. The walls were whitewashed stone, and on one side was a large window with a pointed arch in which glass had been fitted. At that moment, the sun must have come out through a cloud, for its light was pouring in through the glass, splashing cleanly on the whiteness on every wall. Through the window she could see the distant outline of the snow-covered landscape, the flecked lines of hedges and fringes of blue in the sky.

"You could live here," said Simon.

Emily nodded. With the sunlight spilling in, it almost felt warm.

"And look at this." Simon gestured at a massive fireplace protruding stubbily from the opposite wall. It too was whitewashed, and was inlaid with a modern metal grate. Emily went over and stuck her head into the recess.

"I can see the sky," she said, hearing her voice boom hollowly. "It's a working chimney."

"The whole room's been restored," Simon said.

Footsteps sounded on the stairs.

"This is brilliant!" Marcus came through the door and pounded down the steps. He was flourishing a pamphlet. "You should see what—" He paused and glanced about him. "Oh, nice room. You should see what I've found in here!" he went on. "It's got everything in it! I've only scanned through, but it looks really interesting, and I was right—there *were* lots of battles. It was Cromwell who destroyed the outer walls. He put barrels of gunpowder in pits under them, and he was going to do the same to the keep because they'd supported the king, but he got called away. Hold on . . ." He flipped the pages of the pamphlet. "Yeah, there was a big battle near the castle. Two thousand men died before the Roundheads took control."

"Really." Simon sounded deeply bored.

"King John laid siege to the castle, too. Earlier, obviously. And Edward the Second stayed here once. How do you think he died? Well, I'll tell you. A red-hot poker up the bum!"

"It says that in there?" Emily asked, surprised.

"Well, no—"

"Marcus," Simon said, "you talk so much crap."

"It's true, I tell you! I swear! I'm not making it up. I read it in a book."

"You read too much in books. What tripe!"

"I'm sure it was Edward. It was so no one could tell he'd been murdered, you see. No obvious wounds. They laid his body out in a white robe and got the sorrowing commoners in to see him looking all sweet and saintly. And no one among all those thousands of mourners knew the evil truth—he'd been horribly bumped off!"

"So how do we know now?" Simon asked pityingly. "If no one knew at the time?"

"Well," said Marcus, looking slightly put out, "someone must have ratted, obviously. They couldn't keep the ghastly secret. Whispered rumors spread and—slowly, gradually—the terrible truth came out."

Simon sighed heavily. "And what's that got to do with our castle?"

"Nothing. Except that Edward was here—a king! Maybe he stood right where we are now."

"So what?" Simon wasn't disposed to humor him, but Marcus refused to rise to the bait.

"And now there's just us," he continued. "No one else. It's perfect! Have you been to Windsor?"

"Yeah, on a school trip," said Emily. Simon didn't answer.

"I've only seen it on telly. It's the biggest castle in England, but it doesn't interest me much. It's too tidy. All comfy and modernized, with satellite dishes and cars parked in the courtyard. Got the Queen in it too, which is a downer. I mean, it's *boring*. The best castles are small—ruined and remote like this one. They may be all empty and desolate, but there's still something . . . I just think they're still living somehow—do you know what I mean?"

"Nope," said Simon. He was looking out the window. The sun had sunk low over the trees of the woods.

"I think I do," Emily said slowly. "They're alive because you can interpret them how you want. They can be anything you choose. You can imagine how they were in the past, when they weren't ruined, when people lived in them. And everyone's free to imagine different things."

Marcus nodded. "Yeah, but it's not *all* about the

past," he said. "There's us—right now. We've taken over this place, and we've got to decide what to do with it. This castle's got masters again."

"Yeah, till nightfall," Simon said. "I reckon we've got half an hour, tops."

"*Half an hour?* We haven't even started to look around!"

"Okay, you can stay longer, and try to climb down after dark. Use your head."

Marcus groaned. "Why didn't we start earlier! What a waste!"

Simon shrugged. "Look, we did what we came to do."

"We've barely scratched the surface. Ah! Look—" Marcus flipped the pamphlet to the middle and opened it. "Look at the map: there are dozens of rooms and staircases left. Check it out! We can't go now!"

"Give over, Marcus," Emily said. "Stop getting so worked up. We put one over on Harris; no one's ever done this—"

"We shouldn't have started so late! It's your fault, Em. If it wasn't for your stupid aunts we could have got going at a sensible time, not two o'clock in the bloody afternoon!"

"Tough! You'd never have got in without me. If it hadn't been for me you'd still have been swinging about like an ape when Harris came round and caught you."

"How d'you work that out? I got up on my own."

"You practically had to be carried up!"

"Get lost!"

"Stop whinging!"

Simon shifted irritably at the window. "Come on," he said. "We may as well go. It's no fun here."

Emily and Marcus both took a deep breath. "But I mean, look," Marcus said in a calmer voice, pointing at the plan in the pamphlet, "there's murder-holes here and everything."

"Murder what?" Simon asked.

"Holes. Cut in the roof of the entrance passage. So defenders could pour boiling oil or fire arrows down on anyone who forced their way through the doors. Imagine that! You'd just sit quietly in the room above, waiting. Then when someone appeared below, you'd tip the vat of oil over and give him a shower of death!"

Simon snorted. "You'd just love that, wouldn't you? So where are they, then, these holes?"

"Over the entrance. We'd need to go explore a bit to find 'em."

"Haven't time. Sorry. Shall we go, Em?"

"What?" Emily had been looking over at the fire-place with its shining metal grate. "Sorry," she said slowly, "I was just thinking. You know, we could really do it—stay here, I mean."

"Yeah!" Marcus said. "Now you're talking sense. We could see our way about for another hour at least."

"I don't mean today. . . ." Emily went on in the same measured voice. "Obviously—we'd fall and break our necks. I mean another time. We could bring sleeping bags and flashlights and food and—"

"It's midwinter," Simon pointed out.

"So we build a fire. That's what that hearth's for, isn't it?"

There was a stunned silence. Both Marcus and Simon were digesting what they had heard. At last Simon frowned. "People will see the smoke from the chimney and come running," he said. "It's a stupid idea, Em. Bad enough to be one of his."

Emily smiled. "They won't see the smoke if we build the fire after dark!" she went on. "We use flashlights to see, then we build the fire and put sleeping bags down around it, and we could even cook stuff on it if we were careful—"

"Em—"

"Besides, there's a gas heater in the hut downstairs. We could use that during the day, and at night too if we managed to lug it up here. Once we're in, like we are today, there'd be nothing to stop us."

"Harris would see the glow of the fire through the window," Marcus said. "He'd catch it a mile off."

Emily crossed to the window and looked out. "No chance. Nothing but open country there—just endless fields. Harris's place is round the other side. Flashlights or fire, no one would see them. We'd have to be careful with lights near the other windows, of course."

Simon still looked dubious. "It's a crazy idea," he said. "We're already risking too much getting in here at all. Likely enough we'll set fire to the place and burn to death, or get ourselves locked away."

Emily grinned at him. "Yeah," she said, "but you'd still love to do it, wouldn't you, Simon? Come on— you're not chicken now, surely."

He flushed. "'Course I'm not."

"Well, then. We couldn't do it without you, of course. We'd never get in or out on our own, would we, Marcus?" There was no answer to this. "And I wouldn't have a clue how to get a fire going, or switch that heater on." She was resorting to open flattery, but Simon seemed oblivious to it. He nodded thoughtfully.

"I *could* carry some wood up," he said. "Dad's got some out back."

"There you go. Come on! This would be the real thing, just what Marcus's been looking for."

As she spoke she looked sideways at him. Marcus's

face was shadowed in the fading light. The more Emily talked, the more conscious she had become that Marcus was not comfortable with her idea at all. Far from leaping on it and claiming it as his own, as she had expected, he was remaining unnaturally quiet. Why this was she did not know, but she found that his apparent discomfiture spurred her on. So much for his boasting, his know-it-all facts, his endless snide re-marks! A heap of petty grievances, which had been building up steadily in her all day and which had been crowned by his latest bout of ill temper, fueled her growing enthusiasm for her plan. When she first spoke, it had been little more than a half-thought, a small spark of inspiration. But the more uncomfortable Marcus became, the more Emily felt that her plan was a good one.

"You *are* up for it, aren't you, Marcus?"

Even in the dusk, he was obviously ill at ease. "Maybe."

"What's up? I thought this was your dream come true."

"Yeah, it's just—"

"One thing," Simon said. "What do we tell our parents? I mean, mine don't give much of a toss until midnight, but after that they start noticing."

"Oh, yeah." Emily hadn't thought of this. True, it was

a tough one. But even as she prepared to give up the idea, she could sense Marcus relaxing at her side. He was getting off the hook.

"Easy!" she said. "We just say we're staying over at each other's houses. Say there's a Christmas get-together or something. With other kids in the village. Would your parents ask questions, Simon? Mine wouldn't."

"I don't know. They'd be a bit *surprised*, maybe. It's not something any of us have done much of, staying out at someone's. Staying out at the pub, now that's different. Still, I don't reckon they'd ask any questions."

"Cool. *So*," Emily went on brightly, "what about you, Marcus?"

He had his hat off and was scratching irritably at his hair. "I don't know," he said. "It's easier for you—you live here. You can cover for each other. What do I do? I can't say that I'm round your house, can I?"

Simon gave a grunt of acknowledgment, but Emily was in no mood to compromise. "Just say you're round at a mate's in King's Lynn. It's not that difficult. Assuming you've got a mate there, that is." There was a pause. She looked at him. "You must have got *some* mates, Marcus, surely."

Marcus said nothing. Emily turned her discomfort into a burst of exasperation.

"Oh, look," she said, "don't worry about it. If you're

not up for it for whatever reason, that's okay. You can stay at home. Simon and I will go."

This produced a more emphatic reaction than she had expected. Marcus grabbed her by the arm.

"Ow! Marcus—that hurts!"

"Not without me, you won't! You're not doing anything here without me. Whose castle—idea was it to get in? Mine! It was mine. I had the idea. Without me you'd still be messing about like kids out there in the snow! So don't think you can swan around in here as if it's yours, all right?"

"All right!" Emily pried his hand loose. Marcus was panting heavily, wild-eyed with distress. "All right. So you're on for it, then. Good. That's all three of us, which is the way it should be. Let's do it tomorrow. No point wasting time."

"What are you going to tell your parents, Marcus?" Simon asked.

Marcus snorted. "Nothing. Don't need to. My dad works nights."

"What about your mum?"

The answer came witheringly. "I don't need to ask her permission, Simon. She's dead."

"Oh."

The sun had almost completely disappeared behind the trees. The snow on Castle Field was stained a reddish purple. They stood silent in the room.

Marcus folded the pamphlet and stuffed it in his coat. "Sun's down," he said. "We'd better be getting off, then."

"I'm sorry, Marcus," Emily said.

"We'd better be getting off, then," Marcus said.

OCCUPATION

5

It was a perfect day for the great operation. Throughout the morning it had been snowing heavily, but by
2:30, when they met again at the gap in the hedge, the
clouds had lifted and lightened, and the chill breeze had
dropped. There was a hushed feel to the countryside;
everything around them seemed muffled. Every branch
and twig was crowned with a delicately balanced layer
of snow. Thin twists of smoke rose up from the houses
beyond the woods. The sky was a dead, dull white.

Since they had little more than an hour to get settled before the light began to drain away, they did not
waste time. Each carried a large rucksack and was
sweating heavily under as many extra layers as could be
worn inside a bulging coat. With barely a word they
squeezed through the hedge one by one and scuttled
the now-familiar route across to the moat and up to
the castle wall.

"You look like the Michelin Man," Marcus whispered to Simon as they paused for breath by the buttress. "How many jumpers have you got on, there?"

"Six. I nicked them off my brothers. And I've got two more in the bag."

"Jammy git, I've only got four, total."

"It's well camouflaged, eh?" Simon said. "You'd have to look hard to spot that." He pointed up at the cord that he had worn around his waist when climbing the wall for the first time. Now it hung down limply from the hole, blending in with the gray and white stone. Its end dangled just above the top of the buttress. Beyond the hole and out of sight, it was tied to the end of the coil of rope. The day before, after Marcus and Emily had descended, Simon had pulled the rope up and hidden it on the broken wall. After leaving the cord dangling, he himself had climbed down the wall and slid down the buttress.

"If Harris is sharp-eyed he'd spot it," Emily said.

"Better than climbing it all from scratch. Watch out." Simon took a couple of steps back before making a short sharp charge at the buttress. He got about halfway up, made a wild grab at the cord, missed, and slid back to earth.

"How did you do that to your face, Marcus?" Emily

was looking at him properly for the first time. "Looks sore."

"Knocked it coming down yesterday."

"Ouch. Told you it was stupid doing it in the dark."

"Yeah. Watch your feet, Simon! Nearly had my eye out."

"Gotcha!" This time, Simon's outstretched hand found its mark. He landed in the snow with the cord in his grasp. Out of the hole, the end of the rope appeared; as Simon continued to pull, the whole length emerged until it hung to ground level. He grinned. "How's that for genius?"

Emily returned from a reconnaissance around the edge of the tower.

"All clear," she said. "Today, I'm going first."

When all three were on the walkway and the rope had been drawn up, Simon shouldered his pack and set off toward the stairs.

"Hold on!" Marcus jerked his thumb along the corridor in the opposite direction. "You're going the long way round." He took the crumpled pamphlet from his pocket and set it on the stone ledge with the castle plan face up.

"Look, we're here. . . . We follow this passage, we join the staircase up to our room. We'll be there in no time."

"Fair enough. Lead on."

After a few meters they passed beyond the arches opening onto the great hall's empty space, and the walkway became an enclosed passage. It went straight on and ended at another spiral stair, with a doorway on the left.

"See, we ignored this twice yesterday." Marcus stepped over to the door. "Our room's above, but there's another one in here. Let's check it out."

A short passage led into an open chamber—larger, but much darker than the one that had been restored. It had no fewer than three other exits, one of which opened into the thin air of the hall. A set of bars and a sagging sheet of netting blocked this doorway off. There was another fireplace, a couple of narrow windows, and a pervasive feel of damp and cold.

"I like our room much better," Emily said. "Come on, let's get up there and dump our stuff."

They turned to the stairwell, Simon leading.

"They reckon that might have been the lord's chamber," Marcus said. "It leads on to the castle chapel. I'd like—"

"Shh!" Simon suddenly froze in midstride.

"—to have seen—"

"Shut up!" His hiss brought Emily and Marcus up short, bunched behind him.

They listened. Emily heard their hushed breathing, a crow cawing on the wind, but no other sound.

"What did you hear?" she whispered. Simon shook his head furiously, grimaced urgently.

Nothing . . .

Then—a faint scuffling on the stairs below.

A low cough, a muttered curse.

Emily's insides became water. Her legs nearly gave way. She couldn't move.

Simon swiveled very, very quietly. He cupped his hands over his mouth. Slowly, deliberately, his whisper came. "Someone . . . Is . . . Coming. Hide."

Panic. Emily had always associated the word with noise, with crowds and kerfuffle, with loud, wild movements, screams, and shouting. But now here it was, most certainly and definitely—an utterly silent panic that froze her brain and made her jaw sag. Time seemed to flow like treacle. She did not know what to do. She saw Marcus turn around with fear etched on his face, she felt him disappear through the doorway into the cold room. She half turned to follow, but was distracted by Simon: first he seemed inclined to go up the stairs—he took two great tiptoe-ing strides, then he stopped. He turned around, shook his head at her, began to follow Marcus, and stopped again. She saw him mouth a swear word. Then he was past her and off along the corridor toward the walk-way.

The scuffling steps on the staircase grew louder.

She did not know why Simon had gone that way. She did not know whether she should follow him. Perhaps, on reflection, she would. She took a step—and out of the corner of her eye she saw a moving shadow curving upward along the wall of the spiral staircase, and knew that in another moment the owner of that shadow would turn the bend and have a clear view to the landing. Then he would see her.

In a flash of decision she took a step back, twisted around, and set off up the stairs.

And no sooner had she done so than she remembered that their room was a dead end. There was no way of escape up there.

But probably the owner of the shadow would not follow her. There were two other routes for him to take. Then it would be okay. She could wait in hiding on the stairs until the coast below was clear.

She paused in the dusk between two arrow slits. *Listen . . .*

Not a sound to be heard. Had he gone else-where?

Still nothing. Emily breathed a long sigh of relief through dry, parted lips.

Then she heard the footsteps climbing onward up the stairs.

Climbing on toward her.

Oh no. Oh no.

She forced herself to lift in turn each deadened foot, heavy and cold as marble. One at a time, one at a time, stealing up the stairs.

Oh no. Oh, God. Oh no.

It was Harris, she knew it was, and when he found her he would kill her. Maybe he knew they were in the castle; that was why he had come. He had come to find her and kill her, and he would do it in the whitewashed room at the top of the stairs.

Up she went, fast as she dared, and then she was at the top, where the black grilles barred the way along the passage, and up the stairs to the door that opened into the room of light. She spilled out into it, looked around. Nowhere to hide.

A wheezing cough behind her, not far now.

Only—maybe—the chimney . . . ? She raced across to it, ducked under. No time to consider it one way or the other. She stepped onto the grate, stood up inside.

Head and shoulders hidden. Not enough.

She raised her hands, gripped on to the brickwork. It was rough, irregular. Seizing with both hands a brick at the front of the flue, she swung her legs up to lodge against the back of the chimney. It was an awkward movement—she was twisted like a cat in free fall, her head facing downward and her feet facing to the side—but it held her in position. Her rucksack shifted on her back under its own weight. Her right hand found a new grip a little higher up. She took it, adjusted the left hand too, then with more freedom of movement, locked her back in an arch and walked her feet a few more steps up the opposite wall. Flecks of black-brown powder drifted to the floor with every shift in position.

Someone entered the room.

Emily stopped moving. She hung there, wedged in the darkness. One side of her face was pressed against the soot of the brickwork. With half an eye she could see down between her wrists to the pool of light coming in through the fireplace. Even to half an eye, the mess of powder on the grate below screamed incrimination.

There was an incoherent sound of footsteps. They halted. Somebody blew his nose loudly and messily. There were a couple of sniffs. Then a cough.

Emily had no idea whether her feet were high enough, whether they were out of sight. She imagined them peeping out at the back of the bright, white hearth, bathed in a circular spotlight. She wished, fervently, that her boots had been painted white for camouflage, instead of being dark brown with a hint of red.

Above all, she wished she had never come back to the castle—never seen it in the first place. Whose stupid idea had it been to come back today?

Hers. She had no one else to blame.

The strain was beginning to tell on the muscles in her shoulders. The top of one arm began to shake. As stealthily as she could she shifted the fingers of that hand to change the position of her muscles. Her fingers scraped the fragile brick. A delicate trickle of powder drifted downward into the open hearth. She watched it fall, spiraling gently in the light.

How could it not be noticed?

Biting her lip, eyes closed, she waited . . .

Waited . . .

Emily opened her eyes. The room outside was very quiet. There was no snuffling, coughing, or scuffling. There were neither footsteps nor the sound of moving clothes. In fact, no matter how hard she strained to detect even the smallest something, there was no longer the feeling of any presence in the room.

Even so, she did not budge.

Five minutes passed. The aching in Emily's shoulders grew steadily more unbearable. Still no sound came from outside. But the more she waited and the harder she listened the less sure she became that the silence was not treacherous. She imagined Harris waiting there, as motionless as a praying mantis, his eyes fixed on the open hearth. He was enjoying himself. He knew where she was. He would wait until she thought she was truly safe, until she came out timidly like a mouse from a hole—then he would seize her.

She held on grimly, though her arms, hands, fingers now were all shaking. Her whole arched back was racked with pain. She felt sick inside. She had been up this chimney for hours, days. . . . She could bear it no longer. . . .

Then her fingers gave way. In a cascade of brick dust and medieval soot, Emily fell into the fireplace, twisting her ankle awkwardly on the grate. She rolled out onto the floor, finishing up on her back, with arms out like the hands of a clock. Her feet lolled in the hearth. A plume of black settled slowly all around.

Through the descending cloud, she saw the wooden ceiling. Nothing else looked down at her—no hateful face. No one came to seize her. She was alone in the room.

She lay there for a long time, gathering her breath, too drained to cry.

After a while she moved, wincing a little from the ache in her ankle. Slowly she got to her feet and hobbled to the window. Slinging her rucksack onto the ledge beside her, she positioned herself gingerly,

looking out at the snow far below. A good way off
beyond the moat several children were playing. They
were close to the hedge, just inside it, hurling snowballs
at each other. Emily watched them without interest.
They were too distant for her to see their faces.

When she heard steps on the staircase again, it awoke
in her barely a flicker of interest. Fine, let Harris come.
She was so exhausted, she didn't much care.

"There you are!"

She looked across. Marcus at the door.

"You've been here all this time? What happened?
No way—don't tell me—you went up the chimney!
Ha-ha! What a mess! You should see yourself—you
look like a scrawny panda!" He chuckled heartily and
came over to the window.

"Budge over."

"Ow! Watch my leg!"

"Sorry. What've you done, twisted it?" He sat opposite her, grinning. Emily had never seen him look quite
so delighted.

"Yeah, and it's not that funny, actually. It's bloody
painful."

"Sorry to hear it. But, Em, we did it! We survived
this round. We should be proud of ourselves!"

"I'm too sore to be proud. And look at me—I'm
covered in soot."

"Wounds are part of war, Em. And we won this battle. Boy, did we win it."

"We nearly got ourselves caught, that's what happened. If I hadn't crammed myself up there I'd be dead meat."

Marcus whistled. "He actually came up here, did he? Superb! You did really well, Em. Really well. That's the closest shave yet. Closer than me. I—"

"Where's Simon?"

"Don't know. But he wasn't caught. Harris—"

"It was Harris, then?"

"Who else would it be? Anyway, he's gone and he didn't find Simon. But guess what he was up to."

"Looking for us."

"Of course not! He doesn't dream anyone could get in here. That's the beauty of it. No, he was checking for birds."

"What?"

"Crows and that. You've seen all the railings and netting and stuff they've got up. They don't want the birds getting into these covered parts of the castle. If they come in here and start nesting, they'll fill it with crap in no time. Harris was doing the rounds, double-checking no fat crow had snuck in over Christmas. I heard him muttering about it. *And* he picks his nose— I saw him from behind a pillar."

"I don't need *all* the details, Marcus. So what happened to you? He came up here and nearly got me. Then what?"

"Well, I went into the lord's chamber. Nowhere to hide there—I'd never have dared try the chimney! But there were two other ways out. So I bolted for the nearest, and guess what? It was a dead end! I nearly wet myself, which was quite appropriate because it was a bog. Just a seat at the end with a nice round hole. But I thought I was a goner because I didn't realize he'd gone upstairs after you. So anyway, I ducked out and through to the next door, and that was much better—it led to the chapel."

"What, it's a church?" Despite herself, Emily felt some of her old energy return. Marcus's enthusiasm was catching.

"Nope, just an empty room with a recess that might have been an altar. Where the lord and lady went to pray. Expect King Edward would have used it too, when he—"

"Marcus . . ."

"Okay. So I went in and thought I'd take a breather. Maybe Harris wouldn't come my way, after all. So I loitered there, and before long I heard him come into the previous room, the chamber. Boy, was I scared! You've no idea."

Emily looked at him.

"Oh yeah, you have. Sorry. Anyway, I crept out through the arch and into the next room, and that was a big one filled with pillars. I could hear him coming, so I dived across and pressed myself behind one of the pillars. Then he came in and I could hear him getting nearer and nearer, talking to himself all the time. He was grumbling about the birds, wishing he could shoot them."

"What a swine!" Emily said.

"Forget the birds—I was standing there in peril of my life! I knew he was going to come round the side of the pillar, but I didn't know from which side. So I made up my mind—"

"Hello." They looked up in shock. Simon was there. He was pale, but grinning. One of his hands was wrapped up in a dirty handkerchief. It was stained with red.

Emily's ankle throbbed as she turned anxiously where she sat. "Simon, what's happened?"

"So I made up my mind—"

"Oh, nothing. Cut myself, that's all."

"How? Come and sit down."

"It's fine, really." Nevertheless, he crossed over and leaned against the wall beside them, surveying the room. "What's gone on here? Someone hide up the chimney?"

"Yes. Me. What about your hand? How did you do it?"

"It's nothing. I was on the rope again. Slipped a bit, cut myself on a rock."

"What were you doing on the rope? You trying to escape?" Marcus sounded incredulous.

"Of course not. I was trying to hide the rope. It was spilled all over the ledge, remember? If Harris had gone that way the game would have been up, wouldn't it? Even if he'd just glanced along the passage from the stairs he might have seen it. So I ran down, grabbed hold, and climbed out over the side. I didn't have time to untie it from the railings, so I just hung there. It was a bit useless, really. If he *had* come by he'd have seen the knot and caught me—but he didn't come, so that was all right."

"How long were you hanging there?"

"About twenty minutes. I was scared he'd be down in the hall when I came up, so I left it as long as I could."

Emily looked at him in wonder. "Twenty minutes! I thought I did well staying in that chimney for five."

"You did enough to get through. So we reckon he's gone?"

"Yes, he's gone, and if you two let me get a word in edgewise I'll tell you about it!" Marcus seemed a little put out. Simon looked at him for the first time.

"Sure, Marcus. So, Emily was up a chimney, I was hanging on the rope—what did you do?"

"He hid behind a pillar," Emily said obligingly, as Marcus was about to speak.

"Fair enough," Simon said. "And you saw Harris head out?"

Marcus sighed. "Yeah, there's a long passage beyond the room with pillars. It leads to the way out. Harris went down it, and I followed. A couple of birds had got into a room at the end, where there's another big flight of stairs. He spent ages shouting at them and waving at them with his stick. There was lots of cawing and feathers flying."

"Swine!" Emily said.

"When he'd shooed them out he disappeared round a corner and I heard some sort of door closing. I hadn't dared get too close, but I know he left because I went back to the room with the pillars and saw him pass under the murder-holes."

"You found them, then," Simon grunted.

"Yeah. They're great. Big enough to chuck really chunky rocks down."

"I'm surprised you didn't try to brain Harris on his way out," Emily said.

"I'd have loved to, believe me, but there's plastic

sheets nailed over them. Having said that, we could probably pry 'em up. They're not too heavy-duty."

"I'm more interested in Harris," Simon said. "So he left?"

"Locked and left. We can relax now."

"About time. We're sure, are we," Emily said, "that we want to go through with this? I mean, it's not too late to leave. We don't *have* to stay the night."

She looked at the others—Simon with his cut hand, Marcus with his bruised face. They looked back at her impassively. Emily shifted, flexed her aching ankle experimentally.

"You're right," she said. "We've gone too far to back away from this now."

6

"I was just thinking," Emily said, as she lounged in her sleeping bag in the half-light. "It was a good thing the snow fell this morning, or Harris would have seen all of yesterday's footprints in the hall."

"Even the weather's on our side." Marcus yawned. "We are masters of the castle. How's the fire going, Simon?"

Simon did not look up from his place by the grate. He grunted noncommittally. For the previous five minutes he had been struggling to light the pile of twigs and pieces of broken wood that he had positioned in the hearth. Despite numerous attempts to get things going with scrunched-up newspapers, matches, and a lighter, he had had no success so far.

"Try the heater," Emily suggested. Earlier, with much puffing and cursing, Simon had lugged this up two full stories from the hut in the open hall.

He shook his head. "Don't want to waste it. If we can get a fire going, that'll do us through the evening. The heater'll be safer when we're asleep. It's only half full as it is."

He resumed scrunching balls of paper. Emily wriggled a little farther into the sleeping bag and considered their home base. Night was setting in. Only a final, feeble slab of light marked the position of the window. The room was thick with shadow, and the door to the spiral staircase had been yawning open, black and cold, until Marcus had recently pulled it closed. Two flashlights were switched on—illuminating restricted portions of the room while inking out the margins. Simon was using his while he worked on the fire; Marcus had his angled down at a book he was reading. Emily had not yet turned hers on.

Despite the dark, the room was already looking homey. The three sleeping bags were arranged outward from the hearth like spokes on a wheel. Each person had a pillow made of some item of clothing; in Emily's case, a thick woolly jumper. Here and there were scattered their supplies of food and drink. It was an impressive collection, despite Simon's contribution amounting to little more than two tins of peaches. When questioned about this, he had wordlessly pointed to the pile of kindling he had somehow stuffed into his rucksack, and even Marcus had admitted that this was a fairly valid excuse.

Between them, Emily and Marcus had amassed the following: four cans of Coke; one old lemonade bottle filled with water; a six-pack of chocolate biscuits; half a loaf of sliced white bread; a third-full pot of jam; an unopened packet of cheddar cheese; a large cellophane parcel of cold turkey; three packets of very squashed crisps (they had been in Emily's rucksack when she landed heavily on the hearth); two oranges (a third had met a sad demise in the same hearth incident); two knives; and a pot of English mustard.

"What've you brought that for?" Simon had asked incredulously when Marcus had proudly revealed the mustard.

"Can't eat cheese without it. I need to hide the claggy taste."

With or without the mustard, it was a creditable array. All they needed now was a warming fire—and the sooner they got this the better, because the gathering chill was already affecting them. Emily could feel it piercing her many layers. Her nose was an icicle; each exhaled breath piped brief swirls of steam into the dusk, and she was beginning to shiver uncontrollably. Marcus had burrowed as deep as humanly possible into his sleeping bag. Only Simon, crouched at the fireplace, still seemed to be functioning at full throttle. He struck a match and held it under the pile of sticks.

"There now," he muttered. "That might just do it. Don't anybody breathe."

A dim glow spread from the center of the hearth. Two crumpled-up balls of newspaper flared along their edges—bright yellow, growing to orange. The light illuminated a thin black latticework of twigs surrounding the paper like a tent. For several seconds the paper burned, then one of the twigs above began to glow. Simon had his hands cupped over the little pile, shielding it from any cold wafts of air from the chimney flue. More twigs took. There was a barely perceptible crackling.

Simon remained where he knelt for several more minutes, husbanding the growing fire. At last he ventured to place four larger stakes of wood on top of the burning pile, then switched off his flashlight and stood up painfully.

"Keep an eye on it," he said. "It's not got hold yet."

"Nice one," Marcus spoke in a muffled voice from the depths of his sleeping bag.

"Well done, Simon," Emily agreed. "Let's have some food."

"Yeah, I need it." He kicked his boots off and sat himself in the mouth of his sleeping bag. "Who wants peaches?"

"I think you'll find you're on your own with that

one." Emily reached for the packet of bread. "Have you even got a tin-opener?"

"Oh. No. Forgot it."

Like a giant caterpillar or grub, Marcus swiveled himself bodily in his bag so that he too was facing the food. A hand snaked out in search of the turkey. "You brought tins and you didn't bring a tin-opener? You're going hungry, then."

"He's just lit the fire for us," Emily said reprovingly as she cut a slab of cheddar. "Share and share alike."

"I know. Only joking."

"I know it was stupid, but I left in a hurry," Simon said. "It was a nightmare earlier. My brothers were suspicious, wanted to know where I'd been going the last few days. I found it hard to shake them off. They were all hanging around the kitchen, hassling me."

"They must know you're with us," Emily said, with her mouth full.

"Carl forgiven you yet?" Marcus asked.

"Oh, he's caned me for a dozen other things since then. Chuck us the crisps. The fight's not on his mind now. Neil's worse—he keeps going on about it."

"Fire's going well," Emily said.

"Pass the mustard over if you're not going to have any."

"Turkey, cheese, and mustard in a sandwich? Marcus, you are foul."

"This is a feast fit for a king, this is," Marcus said. "And rightly so. This must be the best banquet here since 1313."

"Why then?"

"That was when King Edward stayed here. This tells you all about it—" He indicated the book open by his side. "I found it in the hut. Gives you lots of stories about the castle, and there are some great ones, I can tell you. Edward came here on a regal tour and stayed with the baron—can't remember his name—eating him out of house and home. It was basically a feast that lasted for a week. You wouldn't believe what they ate: dozens of cows, sheep, and pigs, all roasted on spits— we haven't seen the kitchens yet, but we should find them—together with braised quails, herons, and—wait for this one—peacocks! They cooked them and then decorated the basted birds with all their tail feathers. And there was a bear, and—"

Emily gasped. "They didn't eat a bear! How horrible!"

"You're making this up," Simon said.

"No," Marcus groaned. "It was a dancing bear! It entertained them in the great hall while they were eating."

"Cool," Simon said.

"It's still horrible," said Emily. "Poor bear."

"Apparently the king and his court ate so much that the baron had to send out to one of his other castles on the other side of the fens to get extra provisions. It practically bankrupted him. And you know what? The king wasn't grateful at all. A couple of years later he confiscated the castle, gave it to someone else, and banished the baron to France. Not fair, eh?" He paused for breath and took a giant bite from his sandwich.

"How come you remember all that?" Emily asked.

"'Cause he invents it," Simon said. "No one would eat a peacock."

"'Cause it interests me," Marcus said with his mouth full. "There are some great stories in here. Some are really spooky. There's one where—Mnnnnnnf!" He fell back in agony, rubbing his streaming eyes.

"That'll learn you," Simon said. "*Mustard with cheese.* Have some water."

"So all your brothers still live with your mum and dad, do they, Simon?" Emily said. "None of them work?"

"Nah. They just clutter up the place till the pubs open. It's crowded. Three of us sleep in my bedroom. Pauline gets one to herself, as she's a girl. Never any peace."

"It's a lot quieter at my place," Emily said gloomily. "Feeling better?"

"My nasal hair's burned off, I swear it! I'll never smell again!"

"You'll smell, all right," Simon said, wrinkling his nose. "Believe me. Some things don't change."

"Ha-*ha*. And a bit of turkey's gone down my bag."

"Just you at home, then, Em?"

"Just me."

"What's your dad do?"

"Accountant."

"La, bloody, da."

"It's not that posh. What about your dad?"

"Nothing now. Used to work on the farms. You know Miller's? Worked there till he knackered his hand in. Industrial accident."

"No! What sort of accident?"

"A tin bath fell on him."

"A tin bath!"

"Don't laugh—or I'll make you swallow the rest of that mustard."

"But what—"

"They were using it for pig feed. Loading it onto a trailer. Dropped it. Fell on Dad's hand. Snapped the tendons. Knackered."

"Poor guy."

"Grumpy old sod, more like."

"What's your dad do, Marcus?"

"*My* dad? I don't know. Don't care. Something at a factory. Works nights."

"He's happy with you being out tonight, is he?"

"Sure."

Marcus picked up his book and began to leaf through it. Emily watched him.

"So what did you tell him in the end?" she asked. "About tonight."

He didn't seem to hear her. He flicked the pages with deliberate care.

"Come on, Marcus," she said. "No secrets tonight. Simon and I've been talking about our families and stuff. What's the problem?"

Marcus looked up. "I haven't heard *you* say anything," he said.

"Well, what d'you want to know? There isn't much to say."

"Well, I've not got much to say, either."

"All right. My family. Let's see . . ." Emily frowned and began to count points off on her fingers. "There's me, Mum, Dad. Don't see much of Dad. He works most weekends, brings papers home and sits in the dining room. Doesn't like being disturbed. Mum's mostly around, watching TV. It's all right. They let me do my own thing, except when the relations turn up; then I have to show my face. Otherwise, I can go where I like.

As long as I turn up for meals, they're happy. That's it. Dull, eh?"

"You're right," Marcus said. "That *is* dull. Must be *awful*, hanging out at home, your mum and dad letting you do what you want."

"Sounds all right to me," Simon said. "You don't get picked on, anyway."

Marcus groaned. "I was being sarcastic," he said wearily. "Okay, what did you ask me? About my dad and tonight. Yeah, I didn't tell him anything. He doesn't know. He leaves for the site at ten thirty tonight and doesn't get back till nine tomorrow at the earliest, by which time I'll be safely home and in the kitchen, making him his breakfast."

Simon frowned. "You cook him breakfast?"

"Yes, five days a week." He looked from one to the other. "I wash his clothes as well. On Sundays. Anything else you want to know?"

Emily was a little taken aback. "No, you're fine," she said.

"I've got a question," Simon said. "It's not ten thirty yet. So your dad must know you're out somewhere."

"Sure he does. He knows I'm at the library. I told him I was working there tonight. For a school project. I lie very well. He thinks I'm a ponce, but he let it go."

"But libraries aren't open till eleven," Emily said.

"Well, he doesn't bloody know that, does he? Never been in one in his life."

There was a moment's silence. "It's an early start for you then, tomorrow," Emily said. "Bring your alarm clock?"

"Yes. Can I have some more of that turkey?"

Conversation ceased. While Marcus continued to eat, Simon struggled out of his sleeping bag and walked over in his socks to place another couple of sticks on the fire. The blaze was flaring nicely. Smoke thinned and vanished up the chimney. A flickering red glow filled the wide mouth of the hearth and cast a constant play of light and shadow on their faces. The rest of the room was black. The heat of the fire was sufficient to warm their faces a little, but had not yet shifted the underlying chill. None of them had taken their hats off, and Emily was still wearing her gloves, which were now greasy from the cheese and turkey.

"Let's put the heater on too," she said.

"Not yet." Simon carefully lowered a large piece of wood onto the fire. "Wait till these catch; we'll get some real warmth then."

He returned to his bag. Marcus had rolled over and was reading his book again, holding his flashlight in one hand. Emily leaned on an elbow and watched the play of the flames. Slowly the fire grew, and with it the heat in the room. Shadows danced on the walls and ceiling.

Time passed. Emily felt warmer and more comfy than at any time all day. She was approaching the lovely, hazy, indeterminate time between wakefulness and sleep, when Marcus suddenly spoke again.

"I was right what I said about battles," he said. "You know, when we were in the gatehouse that day. There've been some great fights here."

Emily's drowsing mind became aware of itself again. There was a discontented grunt from Simon's direction, suggesting he had been in a similar state of relaxation.

"The biggest battle was when King John came here to attack Baron Hugh," Marcus's voice went on. "The barons were rebelling against the king's authority and John wanted to sort them out. He motored up here in 1215 and set up a monster siege. Hugh and his men and all the locals were penned up inside the castle walls with enough provisions to keep them going for six months if necessary. The king dug himself in around the moat. He had an army of two thousand men, while Hugh only had four hundred. The king told Hugh that if he surrendered forthwith he'd just confiscate the castle temporarily. Hugh would be banished forever, but his son Roger could inherit it when he came of age.

"Well, that wasn't good enough for Hugh, who hoped that some of the other barons would quickly come to his aid. He rejected the proposal and settled down for the siege. John was furious and launched an attack the very same day. His men tried storming the gatehouse across the bridge, but Hugh's archers cut them down. The moat around the gate was choked with bodies and the water ran with blood. It was hopeless trying to get in; the bridge was the only place where the moat was spanned and it was just too well defended. So John had to sit back and wait. Months went by."

"What about the other barons?" Simon's voice asked from the direction of his sleeping bag. "Did they turn up?"

"No, they didn't. John hadn't needed all his men for the siege, so half his army had gone off and mopped up some of the other rebels in neighboring castles. Hugh was trapped, completely isolated. But he didn't give up hope. He still reckoned that John might get bored or be called away or something. Every day Hugh toured the battlements, talking to his men, encouraging them to constant vigilance, telling them that help would come. His little son, Roger, would go with him. He was only twelve years old, but really brave, and everyone in the castle loved him."

"Maybe this was Roger's room," Emily suggested. "It sort of feels like it might have been. A nice room for the lord's son, somehow."

"Go on, Marcus," Simon said. "So what happened? Did John find a way in?"

"*He* didn't, but someone else did it for him. Some monk reckons it was the worst act of treachery he'd heard of in the history of England, which sounds a little steep, I reckon, but—"

"Get on with it!"

"Okay. Hugh and his men held out for six months, by which time the stores should have been all gone. But they'd been prudent, they'd used them up sparingly, so there were still some left. The water was fine—they had the well. Two more months passed and by now nearly all the grain was gone. The salted meat had been finished long before, and people were starting to get very weak. A few of the old men and women died, and there was talk of killing the horses and dogs and eating those. Well, Hugh was still adamant that there would be no surrender—he knew what would happen to him if he fell into the king's power. But not all of his men felt that way, and one of them was the steward, Hugh's right-hand man. He took a look around and saw everyone in the castle beginning to starve, while outside the walls the king's camp was fixed as permanently as the fields and the forest. Winter was not far off, and he thought it was crazy to let this go on any longer. So he decided to help John win."

"Sounds a sensible man," Emily said.

"Get off!" Simon retorted. "He's a traitor."

Marcus chuckled. He was enjoying the effect his story was having on his listeners. "He *was* a traitor," he said. "And this is what he did. He got some of the guards at the gatehouse on his side, and with their help, smuggled a message out to the king's camp. He promised to open the gates on an agreed date, provided he and his friends were spared when the army broke in."

"What a git," Simon said.

"Well, the king agreed, and the very next night the steward slipped down to the gatehouse before dawn. He and his men killed the guards who weren't in on the plot, then they raised the portcullis and unbarred the great door. When all was ready, the steward lit a torch in one of the gatehouse windows—that was the signal to the king.

"No sooner had the torch been raised than horns were blown and John's army charged over the bridge, through the defenseless gatehouse and into the castle bailey. The defenders sounded the alarm, but it was too late for the soldiers on the outer wall. Before they could regroup, arrows were raining into their backs, and the king's men were running through the houses and stables, setting them on fire and killing the panic-stricken inhabitants as they ran out."

"All this happened here?" Emily said, aghast. "How awful!"

"This is brilliant," Simon said. "So what happened—was Hugh killed?"

"There's one more twist," Marcus went on. "Hugh and his family were all here in the keep when the enemy broke in, of course, and Hugh immediately gave word that the keep's doors were to be secured. He reckoned that John might capture the outer walls, but he wouldn't be able to break into the keep itself. So while the buildings outside were burning, Hugh climbed one of the towers to join his men, who were firing arrows down on the soldiers below. On the way up he paused only to send for his son, Roger, whom he wanted close at hand. Well, after a while, he realized that Roger hadn't turned up, so he sent for him again. Still he didn't show. This wasn't like him—normally Roger was the first at his father's side. So Hugh went down and discovered all the servants hunting high and low—but no one could find Roger anywhere.

"Greatly concerned, Hugh returned to the battlements to resume the resistance, but he hadn't been up there more than a minute when he saw a sight that made his blood run cold. Can I have a sip of water? My throat's getting dry."

"No! You can't!" Simon roared. "Keep it away from him, Em, till he finishes the story."

Marcus grinned. "I'll hurry it up, then. Well, the sun had risen by now, and light was spilling into the burning courtyard. Hugh was looking down from the battlements, and he suddenly saw what he most feared. There, lying in the mud, was his little son. He was wearing his nightshirt and he had his sword in his hand. But he was dead—lying in a pool of blood. He'd been run right through!

"Hugh knew then what had happened. When the alarm was raised, his brave son hadn't waited, but had grabbed his sword and left the keep to meet the danger head-on. Before he'd got ten paces, one of John's men had cut him down.

"When he saw this, Hugh gave a new order and his men followed him. They left the battlements, charged down through the keep, and burst out of the door to take their revenge on the king. It was a final gallant gesture of defiance, but it was hopeless, too. In a moment Hugh was down, shot through the throat with an arrow. His men were either killed or cornered. A few minutes later the survivors surrendered. The great siege was over. When everything was quiet, John himself entered the castle."

"You mean he wasn't even taking part?" Emily said. "What a coward!"

"That wasn't John's way. But he did do one good thing."

"What?"

"He sent for the treacherous steward and his friends. They were just about the only men in the castle who weren't dead or injured, and they were pretty pleased with themselves since their plan had been so successful. 'So,' said John. 'I suppose you are keen to enter my service now?' The men said they were. 'Well,' John continued. 'Just as every lord in the land must swear allegiance to the king and never betray him, so every man must swear allegiance to his lord. Your lord betrayed me and he has paid the price for it, but you in your turn betrayed him. And a man who betrays his master proves one thing only—that he is not fit for office, trust—or life.' At this, the steward and his friends flung themselves on their knees and begged for mercy, but to no avail. They were dragged away and put to death."

Marcus finished in a tone of great satisfaction.

"That seems a bit harsh," Emily said. "I mean, I know they were pretty bad, but they did help John take the castle."

"No, they deserved it," Simon said.

"I don't know . . ."

"Good story, wasn't it, though?" Marcus said. "That

was the only time the castle's ever been taken. By treachery. There were a couple of other sieges, apparently, but the castle held out both times."

"And all that happened here. . . ." Simon lay back with his hands behind his head. "Imagine looking down from the tower and seeing your son lying dead."

"Which tower was it?" Emily asked. "Might be the one up our stairs here."

"Don't think anyone knows."

"Pity we can't get to the top."

"Hold on." Marcus fumbled in his bag and brought out his crumpled pamphlet. "I think . . . let's see . . ." He peered at the castle map in the light of his flashlight. "Yes, one of the towers *is* still open. The one on the opposite side to here. Don't know whether it'll be locked now, but we could go and see sometime."

"Let's go now," said Emily, who was getting a bit hot and itchy in her sleeping bag. The fire was heating the room very effectively. "Why not? It won't take long."

"It'd be a tad cold," Simon said. "Can't it wait?"

"I won't be able to stay tomorrow," Marcus said. He pulled his sleeping bag down and began to wriggle out of it. "Come on—it'll be really creepy in the dark."

Emily followed suit. Simon groaned but complied.

"Just when I was getting comfortable," he said.

7

They fixed themselves up with shoes and extra layers. Simon put the final pieces of wood on the fire, then joined them at the door. All three carried flashlights, Marcus directing his onto the map in his hand.

"Okay," he said. "We're leaving home base. We've got two possible routes. When we get to the floor below, we either go round the keep by the walkway and past the kitchens, or through the chamber and the chapel."

"Which way's warmer?" Simon asked.

"They'll both be as cold as each other. But the chapel route will be more undercover, in case it's snowing or something. Let's go that way. I'll be able to show you the murder-holes too."

"Close the door quickly," Simon said. "Keep the heat in."

Marcus swung the door open and stepped through into the pitch-black stairwell. His flashlight lit up the creamy stones of the central pillar—they shone coldly in the weak light. He set off down the steps, followed by Simon and then Emily, who shut the door behind her.

"Don't let the light show through the windows," she whispered. "You never know if someone will be watching."

"We're safe here," Simon whispered back. "It's the other side that faces the village."

"Even so . . ."

Down the staircase they went, the freezing air biting at their faces. Simon and Emily followed Marcus's black shape, which was outlined in the bobbing movement of his light. On the next level he turned to the right and went down the passage that led to the lord's chamber. Here he swung the flashlight around, illuminating the fireplace and the barred arch that led into the vanished hall. Marcus didn't linger. He ignored an archway on the right—"That's the bog," he hissed over his shoulder—and ducked through one leading straight on. It opened out immediately into a smaller room.

"The chapel," he mouthed.

"Why are we whispering?" Simon whispered.

"Don't know."

"Well, shall we stop?"

"Might as well."

However, this was easier said than done. The castle enclosed them. Its silence was so absolute that it seemed an act of violence for anyone to raise their voice. All three were used to the quiet of the countryside. But that quiet normally held some sounds within it: the hum of a distant road, the noise of farm machinery, birdcalls, wind in the trees. Night silence normally contained sounds too: owl hoots, lonely cars, barking dogs, or, again, the tireless wind. Here inside the castle the separate silences of the countryside and the night were combined and deepened, and although it did not oppress them, it made them cautious and respectful. They walked carefully, slipping along softly, like thieves in a slumbering house.

Simon and Emily anxiously followed the meander of the flashlight beam, watching Marcus's breath frosting up in front of it. He led them through the chapel, under an arch and into a room of uncertain shape and size. It contained several pillars made of rounded stone blocks. Marcus shone his flashlight upward.

"The roof's come away here," he said softly. "You can see the stars."

Where his flashlight was pointing, the ceiling ended in a black gap.

"Move your flashlight," Simon said. "I can't see the sky."

Marcus swung the flashlight beam down—and

something sliced through it, a descending blur of movement. The air shifted in front of their faces. Marcus and Emily both cried out; Marcus dropped the flashlight. There was a crack. The light went out.

Darkness. Silence.

"It's all right, you cretins," Simon's voice said. "It was a bat. Maybe two of them."

"Never mind what it was." Marcus's voice sounded shakily from somewhere near the floor. "Put your bloody flashlight on. I can't find mine."

"You can see the stars now, if you look."

There was the faintest suggestion of light in the formless, dimensionless dark; countless pinpricks, which Emily found that she could see most effectively if she held her gaze a little to one side of their center.

Marcus's voice came again. "Very nice. Now, about that light . . ."

Emily switched her flashlight on. Marcus swooped on his flashlight and picked it up.

"Drat, it *is* broken."

"Never mind, we've got two more."

"Yeah, but it's my dad's. What if he needs it?"

"You can get it fixed. Come on."

"Give us a light, then. I know the way." Marcus took Emily's flashlight and proceeded past the pillars. He angled the beam toward the floor, centering it on two black, circular holes in the flagstones. "Murder-holes," he said briefly and passed on.

They followed him into another long passage. Marcus's flashlight lit the walls on either side, the light accentuating their texture. Emily imagined how this passage must have looked when the castle was new, lined with burning torches and filled with smoke and golden light.

There was still no ceiling above them. "Careful," Simon called to Marcus. "You're blasting that light into space. Someone might see it now. Can't you turn it off?"

"No." Nevertheless, Marcus now held his hand over the flashlight, blocking off the beam except for a semi-circular trace that spilled across the floor to guide his feet.

At the end of the passage was a large room complete with the roof, which Emily could only vaguely sense because of the restriction on the light. There was a wide spiral staircase ahead and several windows in the wall.

"See this?" Marcus directed the light back at a thick wooden door. "That's the way out. Sloping staircase down to the entrance. But we're going up."

He paused. "Let's get on the stairs, then I'll turn the flashlight off," he said. "Too much chance of us being spotted with all these windows."

Once they were on the spiral steps, their arms out-stretched between the left-hand wall and the central pillar, Marcus clicked the switch and blackness swallowed them. After a moment to acclimatize, they began to climb.

In the utter dark it seemed to take forever. Emily's straining senses were reduced to hearing the scuffling of their feet and feeling the smooth, cold stone with her gloved fingertips. The winter air burned her face. Above her, she heard Marcus cough. With nothing to see, her imagination began to invent things of its own. She heard something shuffling along behind her, she felt a breath tickling her neck—

All of a sudden the footsteps ahead ceased, and a moment later she collided with Simon's stationary back.

"What's up?" she whispered.

"The wall on the left's disappeared. Took us by surprise a bit. But it's all right, we're on the next floor. We have to carry on up, I think."

The scuffles resumed and they continued to inch themselves upward step by step. Emily's eyes ached with staring into the darkness. Once, a warm yellow point of light appeared on the left. She knew it was a far-off house and that she must be seeing it through a window, but it was impossible to get any fix on it—it glimmered and glazed and danced in her eye like a will-o'-the-wisp until her head swam. Then she passed by and it was gone.

"I've come to the door." Marcus's voice whispered in the void. "Hold on a sec."

There was a pause.

"Found some sort of latch. Can't work it out . . ." A muffled curse floated down. "Come *on*, blast you . . ." A heavy crack sounded, of metal and wood moving suddenly. Emily felt a freezing draft of air and heard Simon moving forward. She advanced again and came out on the roof of the tower.

A black dome set with clear, hard stars arched over their heads. Its immensity made Emily gasp—that, and the scouring of her skin by the midnight, midwinter air. The cold here was cleaner and sharper than the chill of the castle. It stung and cleansed her as she gazed upward, gulping infinity in. For a moment, her mind expanded with a sense of the scale of space and her own terrible smallness and insignificance. For a fraction of a second she glimpsed a universe in which she might well never have existed, though the same stars shone coldly on. . . . It was a glimpse only; her mind could not hold it and she lost the insight almost as soon as it began. Breathing deeply, she lowered her head. The shadowy outlines of Marcus and Simon were imposed upon that of the battlements. Beyond them were clustered the distant lights of the village, looking soft, loose, and yellowish next to the icy precision of the stars.

She went to join them, her feet crunching on frost.

The landscape was sealed up in darkness, inaccessible except for the vaguely undulating top of the woodland marked against the lowest stars. Far away to the left, a distant glow against the sky signaled the presence of some larger town.

"Beautiful," Emily said.

"Bet Hugh stood here," Simon said. "Waiting for the king's army to arrive."

"Wondering if help would come before the enemy," Marcus added. "Studying the trees, looking for signs of their approach—startled birds, smoke in the forest, campfires at night."

"We're so high up," Simon went on. "He'd have felt safe, wouldn't he?"

"He'd feel the stones under his feet, feel their strength like we can," Marcus said. "Nothing could get in without his say-so. The castle would survive forever."

"And it *has* survived," Emily said, "though Hugh didn't. And it's still strong. Close your eyes and you can imagine the same for us—safe inside, shutting out the enemy."

"We don't have to close our eyes," Marcus said. He was silent for a time.

Emily tried to work out which of the lights came from her parents' house, but found it impossible to guess where their road was. The nighttime landscape had few distinguishing marks. It was a world away from the low, drab, everyday flatness of the fens. Marcus was evidently thinking on similar lines.

"It's like a wilderness out there," he said. "I wouldn't be surprised if wolves or bears came out of the forest now."

"Or robbers," Emily said. "Outlaws."

"King John was the one against Robin Hood, wasn't he?" Simon asked.

"Yeah. Most outlaws would cut your throat, probably, not let you go."

Simon laughed softly to himself. "I was just thinking," he said. "I'd love to see Carl's face if he saw us up here. And Neil's. They'd be messing about down in the moat and suddenly they'd hear a whistle. They'd look this way and that, not know where it came from, hear it again, then—out of nowhere—a snowball from on high. Knocks them down."

"Or an arrow," Marcus said.

"They wouldn't know which way to run, would they? I'd love that." He laughed again. "Hey, maybe they'll be along tomorrow. Wouldn't that be the best? Oh, I'd love it if we could ambush them. I'd love it."

Emily interrupted. "Yeah, but we don't want anyone to know we're here, do we?"

"Well, we haven't got any missiles stockpiled," Marcus said. "Or supplies of food. Anyway—" He peered at his watch, couldn't make out the time, gave up. "—I've got to go first thing."

Simon pressed a button on his own watch and illuminated the face. "Ten past twelve," he said.

"The witching hour." Marcus pushed himself away from the battlements. "Come on, let's go back. Think of that fire waiting for us."

DISCORD

Back in their chamber the fire was dying, but its warmth lingered, and its red glow seemed like a bright light. They dived into their sleeping bags in good spirits. Simon mentioned the heater again.

"I can't be bothered to fiddle with it now," he said. "Shout if you get cold."

"I'm glad to be back here," Emily said. "The tower was amazing, but getting there and back was a bit creepy. Too many gaping doorways."

"It would have been worse if you'd known about the ghost," Marcus said unexpectedly.

"Don't, Marcus—" There was a note of alarm in Emily's voice. "I'll never get to sleep if you make up something horrible."

"I'm not making it up! There's a ghost in this castle. Allegedly."

"Not interested!"

"I'm up for it," Simon said. "As long as it's not boring."

"It's not. It's terribly bloody. But Em doesn't want to hear it."

"Oh, *Em* . . ."

"All right—but don't blame me if I keep you awake the rest of the night."

"Cool. Fire away, Marcus."

"Well. The story goes—are you sure you want to hear this, Em?"

"Yes!"

"The story goes that some lord or other—not Hugh, I think it was after his time, but anyway, the lord of this castle was very lavish. He spent all his money on wine and women, and he was soon deeply in debt. Well, there was one person he knew who could lend him the cash he needed, and that was the abbot of the local monastery. The abbot was well known for being very rich and very wicked: he made quite a business of lending money to people and then charging them exorbitant rates of interest. Anyone who didn't repay him was in trouble—they were imprisoned or beaten up by the abbot's men—and the abbot liked to boast that one way or another, *he always collected his due*."

"What's an abbot doing lending money?" Emily interrupted. "I thought they were meant to be holy."

"Not this one, he wasn't. He was rich and evil. Anyway, the lord sees no other way for it but to borrow money from the abbot. After all, he thinks, I'll soon find some means of repaying him. Well, the abbot pays the lord's debts, and everyone's happy. But all too soon the time came for the lord to pay him back, and the lord was racking his brains to know what to do, because of course he still hadn't any money.

"When the lord failed to cough up, the abbot sent a few messages to remind him, but to no avail. Finally he threatened to take the lord to court if he didn't get his dues by the following week. The lord replied hastily to say that all was settled, he'd got the money at last, and would the abbot come—in secret—to the castle to receive it."

"Why in secret?" Emily asked.

"Because he didn't want anyone to know he was broke, I suppose. Do you want me to tell the story or not?"

"I'm waiting for the bloody bit," Simon piped up.

"It's coming. So, one dark night, the abbot arrives alone at the castle gate. He's wearing a monk's cowl over his face so no one recognizes him. Well, the lord welcomes him in person and ushers him up to his private apartments. In they go together, and the lord shuts the door."

Marcus stopped. Emily and Simon waited.

"Yes?" they both said, almost in unison.

Marcus spoke deep and slowly. "The abbot was *never seen again*. Afterward the lord swore that he'd paid him his money and shown him out later that night, and no one could prove any different. But suffice it to say that no trace of the abbot was ever found. Some people thought he'd been killed by robbers in the forest, but most had other ideas. But the lord didn't care. He'd paid off his debts.

"Years passed. The lord took to spending all his time at other castles. He didn't come back here very often, and when he did, it was noticeable that he never stayed the night. But late one winter evening, he's held up on the road by storms and snow. This castle is nearby; reluctantly he agrees to come here to get food and rest. After eating, he retires upstairs to his chamber—"

"Not this one," said Emily. "Don't say it's this one."

"Doubt it—it's a big castle. Well, it's a stormy night. The wind's howling outside like the voices of the damned. But all is quiet in the castle, until some of the servants are woken by the sound of a scream. They run out into the hall and look up—there on the balcony above stand two figures. One is the lord—he is retreating backward, babbling, talking, pleading, though the servants cannot hear what is being said. The other figure is a little way behind him and is silent; his face always seems to be in the shadows. But the servants can make out that he is wearing some sort of cowl. Well, by now the lord had stopped talking and he's retreating in silence, and the other figure is still coming slowly after him. At last the lord backs himself into a corner; he's right on the edge of the balustrade above the hall. He looks left and right, but there's no escape. . . . Then the cowled figure makes a sudden rush. The lord screams, lurches to get away, loses his balance—and falls! He lands on the flagstones far below, splattering them with his blood. The servants race over, but he's dead—his neck broken. And when they think to look up again, the figure on the balcony is gone, and no one who afterward came running into the hall can remember seeing any sign of it."

Emily shivered in her sleeping bag. "Is it me, or is it suddenly really cold in here?"

"It's you," Simon said. "So—did they ever see the abbot's ghost again?"

"Not that I know of. No need. He'd got what he wanted."

"What about his body? Was it walled up somewhere in the castle?"

"It was never found. Maybe it's here still. . . ."

"Marcus!"

The fire had become a few glowing embers that let out no light. Simon's voice sounded from near them. "You tell good stories, mate," he said.

"Cheers."

"Didn't you say you'd seen a ghost once?"

A slight pause. "Did I? Don't think so."

"You did, the other day. Didn't he, Em?"

"Yeah. In the gatehouse."

"I don't remember. . . ."

"Oh, you were probably making it up," Emily said. She shuffled herself in her sleeping bag. "Well, I'm going to sleep. If I *can*, after that story."

"Yeah," Simon said. "'Night."

A small voice, quite unlike Marcus's normal excitable gabble, came from the darkness. "I wasn't making it up," it said. "I *have* seen a ghost. I'll tell you if you like, but you have to promise not to tell anybody."

There was a silence. Something about his tone made them pause.

Emily said, "You don't have to if you don't want to."

"Yeah," Simon said. "'Course not. But we wouldn't tell, would we, Em?"

"No . . ."

"The thing is, I haven't ever told this to anyone, I've kept it to myself all this time. . . . I couldn't bear it if it got out, I'd kill myself. You understand? Oh, I don't know . . . you'll probably just say I'm making it up. That's what you usually do."

"Not if you swear it's true," Simon said.

"You *can* trust us," Emily said. "But if you don't—"

"No. Okay. I'll tell you. There's no story to it, really. Not a proper one. Okay . . ." He took a deep breath. "Well, it was last year, when my mum was still around. I'd had a row with her, not anything important, just about keeping my room clean. Stupid, really. She got angry, I got angry; I stormed out. Got on my bike and rode off into the country; went along furiously, lashing the pedals, swiping with a stick at the hedges as I passed them. It took ages, but eventually I'd whipped the anger out of me and I turned for home. I was cycling along when I turned a corner of this lane and saw a black figure wearing ragged clothes lurking behind the hedge. I started, swerved, and hit a rock in the road. Went right over the handlebars, landed on the opposite verge, head on the grass, feet in the hedge. I was lucky—lots of cuts and bruises, nothing broken, but my bike was a write-off. The front wheel was all bent. I got up, picked up the bike, and looked over at the hedge where I'd seen the figure. . . ."

"Yes— What was it?"

"It was just a scarecrow. But as I say, my bike was knackered. I was miles from home on a lonely road. So I set off, wheeling the bike, limping along. Took me an hour and a half before I got to my street, and by that time I was in a much worse mood than when I'd set out. I was worn out, sore all over, I'd ruined my bike. . . . When I got to the drive I saw Mum standing in the front garden. She called my name but I was far too mad to listen. I just glowered at her and wheeled the bike away down the side of the house. As I went past, she said, "It'll be all right, love," but I ignored her. Chucked the bike down in the back garden and stomped upstairs.

"Well, I had a wash, put Savalon on my cuts, changed clothes. Felt a bit better, so I went downstairs to make it up to Mum, but I couldn't find her in the garden or the house. She'd obviously gone out. So I sat down with some crisps to watch TV. A little while later Dad came in. He worked day shifts then, but he wasn't due back—he was early. I looked and he was crying. He'd come from the hospital. Mum had collapsed in the garden—a hemorrhage—been spotted by the neighbors . . . Well, she'd died."

"Oh, Marcus—"

"Funny thing was, though, he'd been at the hospital half the afternoon. I worked out the times later. The ambulance had been called only twenty minutes after I'd first set off on my ride, and my dad had got to the hospital fifteen minutes after that. Been there ever since. He'd rung home at once, he said, but I wasn't in.

144

Didn't know where I was. He gave me hell for that later, as if I didn't hate myself for it enough." Marcus's voice dropped away. "Well," he said, "Mum had lingered for a bit, then she'd gone. He'd been at her bedside another hour before coming home—never once thought to ring me *then*, of course. Anyway, you know what I'm saying, don't you?"

There was silence. Emily couldn't think what to say.

"About the garden and the time—"

"Yeah, sure, Marcus . . ."

"Yes," Simon said. "Of course." He cleared his throat noisily.

"'It'll be all right, Marcus,' she said to me."

"Yes."

Silence again. Emily lay on her back, her hat pulled down low and her sleeping bag zipped up to her chin. Through three pairs of socks, her feet still felt chilly, but it was too cold and dark to think about unzipping herself to add an extra pair. She stared at nothing for a time, the blackness swirling around her like a living thing.

"Marcus," she said at last.

"Yes?"

"I was thinking—about what your mum said."

"Yes."

"Just . . . Has it been all right?"

"No, of course it bloody hasn't. Go to sleep."

9

The pale, strong light of day filled the room to its
remotest corners. Emily opened one heavy eye. There
was a pain in her head. Her nose was cold and dripping.
She tried to lift an arm to wipe it, only to find that she
had shoved both gloved hands inside her trousers in a
search for extra warmth. She wrestled one arm free and
wiped her nose with her sleeve, removing one source of
irritation. There were plenty more. Her back had
responded to its night on the floorboards by developing
a dull ache. Her hat had slipped off in the night and left
her head exposed to the wintry draft that was blowing
between the window and the door. Her neck, when she
moved it, was stiff, and her lips were dry and cracked,
and stung when she moistened them.

Outside, the wind was hammering on the window-
pane.

Close by, someone was snoring.

She groaned to herself and with some difficulty unzipped one side of the sleeping bag. Then she sat up clumsily and took in a depressing scene. The once-pristine room, all sunlight and whitewash, was no more. The floor was stained with ashes and charred fragments of wood, which had been blown out of the fireplace at some stage of the night by a gust down the chimney. Alongside this was another layer of detritus, comprising three sleeping bags, sundry boots and other items of discarded clothing, an open book, and (worst of all) a hideous array of half-eaten foodstuffs: torn crisp packets, small chunks of cheese, scattered orange peels, an opened mustard pot, dirty knives, and a cellophane wrapper with a mangled piece of turkey. Adding to the unpleasant picture were the two tufted heads half poking out of their respective bags. Marcus had his mouth open; Simon's mouth could not be seen, but it was probably responsible for the gasping snores.

Emily rubbed her eyes and looked at her watch. It was 9:20. A certain muffled feeling in her head suggested that a cold might be coming her way. She felt lousy with lack of sleep, having remained awake for at least an hour after the other two had dozed off. It was Marcus's last story that was to blame for this: it had buzzed endlessly to and fro like a hornet in her head, populating the darkness with ghosts.

Something nagged in her mind. Something about Marcus . . . not the story exactly, though that still disturbed her. She wasn't sure quite what.

Stiffly, she got to her feet and began to search blearily amongst her scattered belongings for an extra pair of socks to warm her toes. In the short time it took to locate one, she managed to stand on at least one piece of cheese, which ingrained itself squidgily into the fibers of the socks she was wearing. After that she collided with a tin of peaches hiding under an empty plastic bag. She swore and hopped a bit, clutching her foot.

Marcus stirred, opened an unseeing eye.

"Time to get up," she said.

As she sat to force the new pair of socks on over the cheesy originals, something caught her eye. It spilled half out of Marcus's rucksack. An alarm clock.

Then it came flooding back to her: Marcus's dad, Marcus's deadline.

"Marcus!" she said loudly. "Get up! We've overslept."

"Whuh?" His eyes, gray-rimmed, remained stubbornly shut.

"We're late. *You're* late."

His eyes half opened. "What . . . what's the time?"

"It's past nine."

"What! Oh my God!" With a frantic flurry of kicks, Marcus propelled his way out of his sleeping bag and the last vestiges of sleep. In a moment he was upright, tottering slightly, and grasping at his hair. He looked at Emily with hollow eyes.

"I forgot to set the alarm! Oh, no. . . . How much past nine is it?"

"Twenty . . . no, twenty-five past."

"Oh, *no*." He gripped his hair as if he were about to rip it out. "He'll be back by now. What am I going to do?"

"Don't panic. How long will it take you to get home?"

"Almost an hour once I get out of this sodding castle. He'll kill me."

Marcus's first cry had interrupted Simon in mid-snore. Now a rather cracked and peevish query issued from the end of his sleeping bag.

"Keep it down, can't you?"

"No, I can't!" Marcus's snarl dissolved immediately into anxiety. "He'll kill me, Em. What am I going to do?"

"There's got to be a way round it." Emily sat with one boot on, one off.

"Just tell a story," Simon said, his face emerging.

"Do what?"

"Tell a story. It's what you're good at. Make something up."

"I *can't*, he'll see through it. What could I possibly say?"

Emily sat forward. "Well, he doesn't have to know you've been out all night, does he? I know! You had to go off early to get food for his breakfast. You'd run out. Eggs, bacon, bread, something like that."

Marcus whacked his forehead with his open palms. "No! That won't work! The shops are just round the corner. I'd only be gone five minutes. And we've got masses of stuff in, anyway!"

"Calm down. Look, let's get things cleared up and keep thinking while we're doing it. Come on, Simon, shift your bum. We need to get moving. You never know—Harris might be about soon."

In a desultory manner they began the great cleanup. Simon reluctantly emerged from his cocoon, complaining loudly about the cold. Emily put on her boots and began rolling up her bag. Between the two of them they quickly gathered up the noisome remnants of the evening's feast, but Marcus remained where he stood, largely useless, caught fast in the grip of terror.

At last Emily forcibly thrust his rucksack into his arms. "Tidy your stuff up! You'll be even later if you don't get on with it!"

"So what? It won't make any difference." Nevertheless, moving with the unseeing jerkiness of an automaton, he stuffed his sleeping bag into his ruck-sack and collected his remaining things.

When they had finished, Emily stood back and considered the room. Even without their clutter, it looked unwholesomely lived in. Ash, food fragments, and—now that daylight was petering in through the window—plenty of obvious scuffs on the floor marked their habitation.

"Oh, dear," she said. "Maybe we should clean this up."

"How?" Simon said harshly. "Got a broom in your bag, have you?" He looked very much the worse for his night on the floor.

"We shouldn't leave it—"

"Who cares? Let's give Harris some work to do. Serve him right! In fact, let's leave *more* litter around while we're at it. Really mess the place up."

This roused Emily to real anger. She knew it was partly simple weariness that did it, but there was also something palpably wrong in the idea of willfully harming the castle.

"You don't mean that," she said sharply. "Shut up and let's go."

"I don't know . . ." Simon grinned at her. "The more I think about it the better I like it. We could write on the walls with charcoal. Something funny. Maybe a bit rude too. That would really give Harris a heart attack. Yeah, and I need a pee. Might as well go here as anywhere. We all could. Choose our corners."

Emily lost it. "Don't be such a thug!" she shouted. "You sound like one of your stupid brothers! Carl would think of doing something like that!"

"Well, maybe Carl has some good ideas sometimes!"

"Yeah, right. He hasn't had one in his life. He's an ape!"

"That's my brother you're talking about—"

"So who were you ripping on last night? Somebody else? Give me a break!"

More insults flew. Simon looked red-faced and ugly. Emily felt the same. Marcus stood by, looking away. Suddenly he stamped his foot and shouted, shocking the others into silence.

"Shut up! Both of you! Of course we shouldn't mess up the room—it's *our castle*, are you forgetting that? Who else has stayed here overnight? No one for three hundred and fifty years. Who else cares about it? No one—they just use it for making money. It's ours, and we're not going to treat it like some tatty ruin like everyone else does."

They looked at him.

"Simon's right," he went on in a quieter tone. "We can't clear this up now. But there's time for that."

Emily said: "No, there isn't. We're finished. We're going. And *you're* late."

She said it like a dagger thrust. Marcus flinched. The confidence drained out of him.

"I'm not going back," he said. "I'm staying here."

Simon shook his head and blinked as if he didn't believe his ears. "Get real," he said. "Who are you trying to impress?"

"I'm not trying to impress anyone. I'm not going home."

"Just because your dad's going to be mad?"

"You don't know my dad."

"Marcus." Emily cut to the point. "There are lots of reasons why you can't stay here, and I'll list them for you, shall I? You haven't got any food, you haven't got any water—don't give me any cock-and-bull story about the well—you haven't got any heating. Well, you've got the heater, but I bet you won't be able to turn it on. Even if you could, it'll last for a couple of hours, no more. You'll freeze to death before you starve—in fact, look at you, you're shaking already. We're all tired, we're all dirty, we all need to go home. Let's just pack it in."

Mixed emotions passed across Marcus's face—anger, spite, and fear among them. His shoulders slumped. His face sagged with disappointment.

"Simon, the heater," Emily said. "You'd better take it back down, or Harris will see it and the game'll be up."

"What? Who cares if it is? We're not coming back."

"*Please*, Simon." Emily tried to smile, but her face felt stiff and heavy.

"Oh, all right. Get out of the way."

"Thanks. He won't know anyone's been here with that gone."

"You reckon. Open the door, then."

Simon hefted it out onto the stair, shifted his hands into a better position, and vanished. His voice echoed upward. "Bring my bag down. I'll meet you at the hole."

He left behind him Emily and Marcus staring at the empty room.

"I'd know someone had been here," Emily said. "It's a right mess."

"Harris might not notice. He doesn't *care*, does he? Not in the same way. He'll think it's birds got down the chimney, bringing soot with them."

"Yeah. Maybe."

Closing the door behind them, they trooped down the stairs to the next level, where they passed along the walkway to the hole and the coil of rope. Below them in the hall they could see Simon struggling to carry the heater into the hut. The wind caught the open door and half shut it on him as he attempted to go past. His curse echoed up to them through the empty castle. Marcus looked away, out at the fields.

"He reminds me of my dad sometimes," Marcus said.

"Your dad—fierce, is he?" Emily said.

"You could say that. He goes ballistic when I go off on my own. Hates it. Doesn't like me having a life. And since this one's overnight . . ." Marcus sighed. "He'll kill me."

"What are you going to tell him?"

"Not a clue. I've never got on with him, Em. I was always closer to Mum, which he hated, of course. Said I was spoiled. Dad and I didn't speak much, and if we did we'd only fight. Mum could calm us both down, but when she went . . . We didn't have any option anymore, did we? Had to get on with it. It's a nightmare. When he comes home he's always knackered and angry; expects me to do everything for him. Won't let me go out. *'I want you here, where I can see you.'* And he hates me reading. Just wants to watch TV, never picks up a book."

"My parents don't, either. But I know what you mean. It must be difficult."

Marcus looked at her sharply. "But not *too* difficult, is that what you're saying? Not dramatic enough for you? You don't understand, Em. It's driving me mad. I can't bear it! I'd do anything to get away from him."

"What are you going to tell him when you get back?"

"Don't know."

"How about blaming me—say one of your friends—me—called you this morning and needed help. Urgently. Wanted you to go round."

"Why?"

"I don't know, maybe I was ill. Had an accident. No, that's stupid."

"Yes."

"Or you went out to the library again—to finish your work. You're really up against it. Exams."

"So why didn't I leave a note? Anyway, he wouldn't buy it. Thanks, Em, but it isn't any use."

Below them she heard Simon's feet crunching across the snow toward the nearest set of stairs.

"I enjoyed last night."

"Yeah."

"Liked your stories."

"Simon doesn't believe them—*any* of them. He practically said so this morning. Said they were made up."

"He didn't say that."

"He did. What about you? Reckon I'm a liar too?"

"Of course not. Look," Emily said, "why don't you give me your number? I'll bump into Simon all the time, but you're much farther away. Then we can meet up. Do something."

Marcus looked at her. "I take it, then, we're not coming back in here?"

Emily thought of her ice-cold feet, her growing snuffle, her overwhelming desire to get indoors and have a hot bath. "Well . . ."

"Of course we're not. Okay. Have you got a pen?"

"Oh . . . No."

"All right, give me yours. I'll remember it. I've a good memory."

Emily told it to him. Marcus was repeating it for the second time when Simon joined them.

"Right," he said, glancing askance at them. "You two first. I'll take the rope off and follow." After a quick look to check the coast was clear, he spooled the rope out of the hole. Without a word, Marcus clambered onto the wall and lowered himself down and out of sight. Simon stood back and picked up his rucksack.

"Exchanging phone numbers?" he said.

"So?" Emily said hotly. "How else are we going to keep in touch?"

"Are you sure you want to? He's barking, you know."

"That wasn't what you said last night." She put on a stupid voice. "'*Great story, mate! Tell me another one, mate!*'"

"You silly posh cow. Go on. It's your turn."

Emily inched her way down the rope, seething with rage. He was such a boor! Such a moron! She couldn't forgive him for his churlish behavior. He was no better than his brother. Worse, in some ways—at least Carl was so obviously obnoxious it made you keep away.

She arrived at the ground. Marcus was waiting there, looking pale and thin. Something about his stance suddenly reminded her of when she had first seen him tossing snowballs in the moat. Something lonely and forlorn.

"You'd better go," she said. "No sense in making it even worse. I'll wait for that grumpy idiot."

"Something happened?"

"It's nothing. Go on. Hope it goes all right."

He shrugged. Then he turned and began to trudge away.

"Hey!" she shouted suddenly. "Don't forget the number."

He called it back, very fast, over his shoulder, came to the edge of the moat and disappeared into its depths. Emily turned back to the castle wall. Out of nowhere the rope came hurtling down in an angry, writhing coil, narrowly missing her and ripping into the snow.

She looked at it with dull, tired eyes, feeling obscure traces of disappointment and relief.

That's it, she thought. We can't get back in. It's over.

FIRST SIGHTING

10

A day passed, then another. If there had been any important events in Emily's life in those two days, they might have pushed the memory of the castle to the back of her mind. She did not really want to think of it in any case. For a start, she blamed it for the head cold that she had developed the minute she arrived home. It had forced her to go straight to bed, which at least allowed her to catch up on her sleep, but it made her feel truly dreadful at the same time. To add to this grievance, the behavior of Simon and Marcus had made Emily angry and unsettled. Part of her would have been very happy to forget them. But she was trapped in bed with nothing to do. Her parents watched television downstairs. She lay alone and dwelt on things.

Of the two of them, Marcus was on her mind most often. Although she was still furious with Simon for his loutish behavior, her simmering resentment had cooled off as soon as she'd had a decent sleep. In retrospect she wasn't quite sure why she had become so angry. With Marcus, however, things were not so simple. She thought about his enthusiasms, his anxieties, and his endless stories, with a perplexing mix of exasperation and concern. He was so *changeable*, that was the problem—you never had time to get a handle on his mood before it altered. He had an underlying agitation that made him hard to be with.

On the second day, someone had rung for her while she was asleep. He had not left a name or a message. Emily had an idea who the caller might have been and was disappointed when he did not ring back. It made her more unsettled than ever.

Behind all this, barely acknowledged, Emily could not shake her memories of the castle itself—the darkness of its corridors, the red glow in the fireplace, the tower with its canopy of stars.

On the third day, her cold receded enough for her to go out after lunch. She walked through the village slush to the edge of the fields and looked out on the desolation of the winter fens stretching flatly into the distance. The sight dispirited her. She did not want to go farther in that direction. She returned through the village center and out the other side, up the lane and into the woods.

Through the trees she caught the gray flash of stone in the distance. It drew her closer, farther than she'd intended to go. She came to a place where she could take in the whole view, buttresses to battlements, tower to tower. She tried to work out which tower they had stood upon and realized at last that it was the nearest, the only one visible that still seemed complete.

It was a mild but blustery day; much of the snow still on the branches of the trees was slipping off slowly, and there was a continual pattering and rustling in the woods. Emily's head was hot after her walk. She pulled off her hat and scratched.

As she turned to go back, she saw Simon emerging from a particularly thick clump of holly trees on the other side of the road. He looked from side to side in a furtive manner.

Emily whistled. Simon jumped.

"What's up with you? Guilty conscience?"

He walked quickly over to her. "You look rough."

"Thanks. Had a cold. Listen—"

"I'm sorry about the other day. I was tired, I suppose."

"Me too. Forget it. So—what are you doing, then?"

"The same as you."

"What do you mean? I've just come for a walk."

He looked at her closely. "*Really?*"

"Of course. This is my first trip out since I saw you last. So what are you doing?"

He took a swift glance back up the road—no one was in sight—and took a deep breath. "Something's going on at the castle," he said. "Or was. Last night. I came up here yesterday about six. Not for any reason—" he added hastily. "Just wanted to get out of the house for a bit of peace. Well, it was dark, obviously. I had my flashlight, but when I got out of the woods I switched it off. You know, a bit like we did in the tower. And that was when I saw it. A light in the castle."

"What? Where was it?"

"See the near tower, the one we went up? See those windows halfway down? It was there. A flash. I saw it again a minute later, passing that big window farther along the wall. A yellowy light moving to the right. Then it vanished like it had been cut off."

Emily furrowed her brows. "Who do you think it is?"

"Well, I don't think it's the abbot's ghost, that's for sure."

"It might be Harris," Emily said suddenly. "If he noticed the mess we left he might have lain in wait, in case we came back. He probably lurked there for a couple of hours until he was sure it was going to stay quiet."

"I thought of that too. It's possible. But I don't reckon it's true."

"Why?"

"Because on my way home last night I went up Harris's driveway. You can cut onto it by nipping round those bushes there." He indicated the hollies he had emerged from. "And I reckon he was at home. The curtains were shut mostly, but I saw his wife bringing plates through into the kitchen from a room at the back."

"You didn't see him, though?"

"No. But she wouldn't be eating without him, would she?"

"I suppose not. So, if it wasn't Harris . . ." She left the question floating.

Simon raised his eyebrows at her. "Exactly."

"But how did he get back in?"

"That's what's been bugging me. He could never climb up without the rope. No way."

"Maybe it's someone else."

"Right, like the whole of the village is queuing up to break in. No, it has to be him. He's worked out some dodge, found some crack to squeeze through. He realized he could do it without us."

"Would he do that?" Emily kicked at a nearby stump, cracking a piece of sodden bark away.

"Of course he would! He'd like it better without us. No one to tell him what to do. He wouldn't be lonely; he's got the fairies to chat to whenever he wants."

"He's not like that—"

"Whatever. The problem is that he's bound to get caught. Sooner or later, and in Marcus's case sooner; he'll walk right into Harris, or some kid will see his bum disappearing up a drainpipe or something. Don't deny it—you know it's true. If he keeps coming back, he'll be caught and we'll all be for it. They'll take him down to the station, and an hour later they'll be round your place and mine. Believe me, I know what they're like. They won't miss a trick with a boy like Marcus."

"It won't happen," Emily said. She had a cold feeling running down her spine.

"Too right it won't," Simon said grimly. "And that's because I'm going in now to flush him out."

"Are you mad? You don't even know if he's there today. You're asking to get caught yourself."

"Not this time I'm not. I've just been spying on Harris again. He's got friends over. There are three cars parked outside his house. He's fine for an hour or two—probably all day if he's having a few drinks. As for Marcus, you're right, he *might* not be there, but I think he is. He isn't capable of leaving it alone."

As they stood there in the woods, surrounded by the

constant swishing, sliding noises of the melting snow, Emily noticed for the first time the bulging rucksack strapped to Simon's back. She had a sudden flash of insight and laughed.

"He isn't the only one," she said. "*We* can't leave it alone, either. You may be right about Marcus getting caught, but that's not the only reason you're going back in. And it's no coincidence that you met me hanging round here, either."

"You don't have to come."

"You're right, but I will. What're my other options? Go home and watch TV? No thanks."

"We're not staying this time. Just long enough to kick that idiot out."

"Sure."

They set off through the margins of the woods until, still overhung by the last black branches, they arrived at the boundary hedge. Here it was thin and scraggy and had been reinforced in patches by strips of poor wire netting. Simon forced a particularly weak-looking section downward.

"Go on, then, hop over."

"In full view?"

"The snow's melting. No one is going to be around. I can't be bothered to skulk anymore. Come on, after you."

They negotiated the fencing and entered the field. The snow was still thick against the hedge, but looser now, and wet. They plowed through the deepest drifts and set off toward the gatehouse bridge.

As they went, Emily said, "Someone rang for me the other day. Didn't leave a message, or say who he was. It might have been Marcus trying to get in touch."

"Only rang once? Didn't try very hard."

Scaling the wall was far easier for Simon than before, since the treacherous ice that had caked the buttress had now melted, leaving the grooves and indentations nicely exposed. Emily bided her time while he climbed, scanning the horizon for danger, but Simon was right. No one seemed to be out. She also checked the snow around the buttress for recent footprints, but to no avail. The whole area was a churned and slushy mess.

Before long the rope was thrown down and Emily climbed up, a little shakily, as her muscles were stiff and out of practice. Her hair was whipped around her face by the wind, which seemed to be picking up speed. Soon they stood on the walkway as before, Emily looking down into the cavernous hall space. The wind whistled past the broken arches at the top of the keep wall. She could see the castle crows hunched gloomily in their shapeless nests.

"No sign of anyone," she said.

"Well, he's going to be tucked up on a day like this. In our room, most likely."

It was a relief to get into the sheltered section of the passage, out of the ceaseless gale. They climbed the stairs to the door, Simon signaling Emily to be silent. At the top, he gently pushed the door open a crack and peered inside. He frowned, and, abandoning all caution, marched right in.

"Not here," he said redundantly.

Emily looked about. "Not up the chimney?"

"Marcus? You wouldn't see for the soot."

"That's a point. Someone's done some cleaning up here. I'm sure there's less mess than when we left it."

"Think so? Well, he's not here now. Let's keep looking."

They descended the stairs, pausing at the junction that led to the chamber. "Which way?" Simon asked.

"This floor first. Might as well be systematic."

They worked their way speedily into the depths of the keep, keeping their eyes open and their ears peeled. They saw nothing, and the only sound was the wind scouring the passages. In chamber, chapel, latrine, and pillared room there was no sign of Marcus, or any that he had ever been there. The room with the main staircase was empty too.

"Lots of ways to go here," Simon said. "Let's split up. I'll check the tower, you see what's through those two doors. One goes to the main entrance, if you believe what Marcus says."

He clattered up the staircase. Emily entered one arch, and found herself inspecting the kitchen that had once served the great hall. It was a dead end. Three brick-lined baking ovens were built into one wall. Ordinarily, Emily would have been quite interested in these, but for now she was impatient to be gone. She retraced her steps and approached the other arch, this one complete with a modern door.

She flicked up the large black metal latch and eased the door back. A very dark staircase—straight, this time—led down steeply. Emily descended and soon arrived at another door. This one was much older, dark with age and pitted with the holes of worms and wear. It swung open loosely to her touch. Beyond it the steps continued, and in the dim light she saw that they were ground shallow and smooth with the feet of centuries. They ended at a short passage of equally worn flagstones, which led to a set of double doors, thickly studded with metal nails. This was the entrance to the keep.

No sooner had she started on her way back than Emily stopped. She had the sudden queasy sensation that she was being watched. She looked up the steps in case Simon had returned, but the distant door at the top was open and empty. No one there . . . But the unnerving feeling persisted. Hurriedly, she stepped forward—

And heard a scraping sound directly above her.

She jerked her head up, her blood running cold. Something on the ceiling?

No—but there were two round holes set in the stonework, deep and dark. The murder-holes. One was right over her, a little wider than her head. She looked straight into it but saw nothing there but shadows.

Marcus.

Emily turned and ran up the staircase as fast as she could, past the second door and up to the first, where she nearly collided with Simon.

"You all right?"

"He's in the room with pillars! By the murder-holes—come on!"

She careered around the corner and pelted back down the long passageway. Into the pillared room she skidded, with Simon right on her heels—

And found it empty.

Simon was gasping for breath. "What are you doing, Em? What made you think—"

"He was here, spying on me through the holes. I

heard him, I know I did. Yes! Look at their coverings. He's ripped them up!"

Between the circular holes were two see-through plastic sheets that had been torn away from the bolts fixing them to the floor.

"How'd he do that?" Simon wheezed. "Must've got some tools."

But even as he spoke, Emily was heading out the opposite door.

"He must have gone this way. Come on, we can catch him!"

They ran back through the chapel and chamber until they arrived at the stairs.

"What do you think? Up, down, or along?"

"Not up—he's cut off there. You go down, I'll go along."

Emily stormed down the stairs, around and around, so fast that she felt giddy. The light grew dimmer as she went. At the bottom she spilled out into the high black storeroom, lit by the arch in the far wall. She began to run toward it, then stopped and spun around, trying to take in the hidden depths of the chamber. It would be just like Marcus to hide here, wait for her to go blundering past. . . .

No—the room was empty.

Out into the daylight. She was back in the great,

open expanse of the hall. The hut was close by, its door hanging open.

There was a shout from above her. Simon was on the walkway opposite, waving. "He *is* here somewhere! I've found his stuff."

"Where?"

"Up the stairs in this corner tower. Doesn't lead anywhere, but there's a stash of things you wouldn't believe! Masses of food, a camping stove, you name it."

"But no Marcus?"

"I reckon he's down there. I'd have seen him if he'd been going ahead of me."

His head disappeared from the opening. Emily strode across the hollow heart of the keep through the melting snow. There were several more archways to choose from, into any of which Marcus might have fled. One led to the room with the well. She tried this first.

Her eyes took a long time to focus in the dim light. The air was damp; water dripped from points across the whole ceiling, splotting and splashing and collecting as puddles in the corners of tilted flagstones.

Emily took a few steps inside to give her straining eyes more of a chance. At first, she could make nothing out; then she began to distinguish a particular patch of darkness that seemed deeper and less remote than everything around it. It was low and lumpish, blue-black against the gray-black of the rest of the room.

Emily moved slowly toward it.

From the lump of darkness came a sudden harsh clashing noise, metal scraping on metal. Emily's heart jolted and she almost turned to flee.

Instead, she heard herself speaking, falteringly. "Marcus?"

No reply came from the blue-black darkness. It moved a little. Another violent clang sounded. Emily shivered with the impact.

"Marcus? Is that you?"

The shape unfolded, became long and slender. A familiar voice spoke testily.

"Of *course* it's me. Who else would it be?"

"What the hell are you doing here?"

"Trying to pry the grating open. I want to see if it's a dungeon."

"Not that. I mean *here*, back in the castle. You'll be caught."

"So might you."

"Yes, but we just came to find *you*, make you see sense. Then we're going."

This time he did not speak. Emily knew he was staring toward her.

When his voice finally came, it sounded odd, with a

hard edge. "Why did you think I'd be here? Who else is looking for me?"

"We—no—Simon saw a light in the castle last night. He guessed it must be you. No one else knows, Marcus."

"You're sure?"

"Of course." There was a commotion somewhere outside. Emily turned toward the entrance and spoke over her shoulder. "Come out of there a minute. I can't talk to you if I can't see you." She climbed out into the light. Simon was waiting outside.

"He's in there, is he?"

"Yes. He's coming out, I think."

"Good. I've a few things to tell him." Simon lowered his voice and leaned close to Emily. "When they see the murder-holes they'll say it's vandalism," he whispered. "And the first people that the police will call on will be you and me, seeing as Harris met us outside so recently. Well," he added bitterly, "they'll call on *me* first, but they'll find out who you are too, believe me."

Emily felt a little sick inside. "Can't we get him to mend the covers?" she asked.

"Mend them? He's busted them good and proper. The only thing we can do is get out sharpish. Ah, here he is," he said, raising his voice. "The defender of the castle."

A slow figure emerged from the lip of shadow under the arch.

"Don't patronize me," it said. It stepped forward into the light.

"Oh, *Marcus*," Emily said.

"Bloody hell," said Simon. "What's happened to you?"

11

Marcus's hat was pulled down low over his brows. A thick woolly scarf, which Emily had not seen before, was wound high around his chin. But these did nothing to disguise, and in fact only served to frame, the enormous blue-black bruises that were disfiguring his face. The worst spread across his left cheek, but there was a smaller, bluish one on his forehead above. Between them, his left eye was completely black, swollen, and half closed. The other eye looked tired and red.

The disruption to his face contrasted oddly with the clothes Marcus was wearing. As well as the jaunty new red scarf, he seemed to be decked out in an entirely fresh set of all-weather gear. He had a large, shiny trekking jacket, decorated in a slightly garish blue-and-orange zigzag pattern. Beneath this showed the top of a thick Aran jumper. His overtrousers were made of the same material as the jacket, and were tucked neatly at the base of each leg into a svelte gray camping sock. These in turn protruded from two very shiny new walking boots.

"Smart, eh?" Marcus said. His face grinned wonkily.

Emily and Simon did not grin. "Marcus—how did you get like that?" Simon said.

"Are you talking about the clothes or the face?"

"The face, of course. And the clothes . . . Just tell us what's going on."

"Your face . . ." Emily said. "Did you slip and fall?"

"Nothing as straightforward as that, I'm afraid, Em. No." His good eye fixed on her beadily from under his flattened fringe. "I told you Dad wasn't going to be happy about me staying out, and happy he certainly was not."

"You mean—"

"It was the lying, apparently, that really got him going, that's what he told me as he locked up my bike. The lying. That was worse, far worse, than the sneaking off, no matter where I'd been. He never bothered to find out exactly what the truth was, but he sure as hell knew when he wasn't hearing it. Oh, it was quite funny when I rolled in and came out with the early morning library story—you remember, Em, the one you suggested. I'm not blaming you: I couldn't think of anything better, that's all. I was listening to myself saying it and watching my dad's hands and thinking to myself, 'I've never heard anything that sounds more like crap in my entire life.' I could almost have hit me myself, it was so lame. And the funny thing was that as I was standing in the hall, rambling on about books and study hours, my dad must have been looking over my shoulder all the time at my open rucksack—I'd forgotten to close it properly when we left here—and seen nothing in it except the end of my sleeping bag poking merrily out. Well, I might as well have had a neon light flashing away on my head saying 'I am a liar,' and he made his feelings pretty plain after that, Dad did."

"But," Emily said, "he . . . he can't do that—"

"Don't tell me what he can and can't do!" Marcus rounded on her savagely. "I know a hell of a lot more about it than you! And that wasn't all he did, either! No, he went off to his shed and came out holding a big mallet thing he uses at work. The kind you knock fence posts in with. Then he went to my bike where I'd left it leaning against the side of the house and laid it out on the concrete slabs by the back door. Proceeded to smash it to scrap metal. Took him quite a while. I timed him: six minutes, twenty seconds. Worked up quite a sweat. But I didn't care. I knew what I was going to do even as I stood there watching him. When he'd finished, he went to lie down—worn out he was, poor man. I carried the pieces to the side of the garden like he told me to, out of the way. Then I went to the bathroom and bathed my face. Had some cereal. Slept most of the rest of the day."

Marcus stopped talking and patted Emily's arm with a newly gloved hand. He indicated the nearby hut.

"You both look a bit cold," he said. "Let's go in there. I've got the heater working."

Dumbly, they followed him into the tiny interior. With the heater, shelf, cupboard, and chair, it was barely big enough for all three of them standing together. Marcus squeezed over to the heater and fiddled with a dial, while Emily closed the door. A low humming noise began, followed swiftly by the smell of burning dust.

"Won't take a minute to warm us." Marcus picked up a packet of biscuits that was lying on the shelf. "Have one. Em—you take the chair."

The biscuits were passed around. Emily sat on the chair, the others on the floor. For a minute they crunched in awkward silence, feeling the generated heat slowly steal over them. Emily shivered luxuriantly as she grew warm, but her eyes remained fixed on Marcus. He now seemed remarkably composed.

Simon took his third custard cream. "So how did

you get down here, then," he said, "if your bike was knackered?"

"I think," Marcus said, examining the fragment of biscuit he held in his hand, "that Dad felt removing my bike from the equation would prevent me from going off again. He's simple that way. I've always cycled places to get myself out from under his thumb, and it's always driven him mad. Maybe this was the worst occasion, but not by much. He hates it if I'm not there when he needs me, or when he's asleep and might wake up and want something."

"I can't believe he hit you," Emily said suddenly, uncorking at last.

"Well, it wasn't that so much. It was the bike . . . Anyway—I won't make this into a long story, so don't worry, Simon—I lay there that day working out what I wanted to do. Next morning, when Dad came home, I was there, as good as gold. Made him his breakfast, gave him his paper, waited for him to go to sleep. He takes pills to knock him out, so I was safe once that was done.

"The rest was as simple as pie. It was all about gathering supplies. I wanted food, drink, heat, maybe a bit of comfort. I thought of Baron Hugh, how he'd have systematically gathered in his corn and livestock before barring the castle door. Which reminds me—I've got a brilliant idea for keeping Harris out, if necessary!" He paused to bite a side slab off another custard cream.

"If armies were in enemy territory, they'd despoil it," he went on. "And that was what I did with Dad. First I took everything I could from the fridge and pantry, which wasn't much because we were running low. A few tins, mainly—and I didn't forget the tin-opener either, Simon, you'll be pleased to know. I could have used some of the breakfast things—eggs, bacon, tomatoes, but hell, I was going to buy them later. So I chucked them in the sink and left them. Opened a tin of beans on top for good measure. Then I went upstairs to Dad's room, found his jacket, and took his wallet. You all right there, Em?"

"Yes. Go on."

"That got me twenty quid. Not nearly enough. But there was his debit card too, and Dad had made a big mistake with that. A while ago, being a lazy sod, he'd got me to go to the hole in the wall and get him some cash. So I knew his number. I don't forget things like that. I took the card and the twenty, and chucked the coins into the sink with the rest. Then I left. Took the rucksack but not my manky old sleeping bag. Walked into town, visited the bank, and did a spot of shopping at Safeway and the Outdoor center. I've got a very nice new flashlight, guys, with settings for three types of beam."

"You didn't buy a new bike, did you?" Simon asked. He was looking at Marcus with a kind of begrudging respect.

"Not enough cash, sadly. Had to take a couple of buses. Got here in the afternoon."

"And how did you get in?"

"But, Marcus," Emily interrupted, "you're not going to stay here."

"Why not? I'm not bloody well going back, and I'm not sleeping in the street, either. This place has got it all, except a water supply, but I can melt snow. I've brought books, heating equipment . . . there's firewood not far away. I'll just need to make a few trips into the village for food now and again, and I won't even need to do that for a bit. I just need to make sure you two don't give the game away, that's all."

"You'll be caught so fast, Marcus," Emily said.

"You are a real doom merchant, Em, you know that? My dad hasn't got a clue where I am, I've not told anyone apart from you, and the castle's shut up till March. I can keep out of Harris's way. I know his route already."

"But how did you get *in*?" Simon persisted.

Marcus laughed. "Easy! Harris let me in!"

"Meaning what?"

"Meaning I was lucky. I stashed my stuff under the

hedge—and was I glad to get rid of it! Nearly broke my back carting it up from the village. I did a recon, and I was thinking I might have to call you again, Em, when—"

"So it *was* you who rang me yesterday. Why didn't you leave a message or phone back?"

Marcus shrugged. His trekking jacket crackled. "I don't know why I rang you, really," he said. "It was when I was about to leave. I was flustered, I guess, and I hadn't a clue how I was going to get inside. I had half an idea that you and Simon might rig up the rope again. But when I couldn't get through, I changed my mind and decided instead just to get out here, see what turned up. I didn't want you to be involved if I could help it."

Simon glanced up at Emily with a "told you so" kind of look.

"Anyway," Marcus continued, "I was just collecting my stuff again when I saw Harris crossing the bridge. Whether he was going into the keep or not I didn't know, but I didn't want to miss my chance, so I wriggled under the hedge and pelted after him at a safe distance. I was at the gatehouse when he got to the keep, and—lo and behold!—before my very eyes he unlocked the door and went in.

"I had to take a gamble here, so I ran to the tower,

fast as I could, and peered round at the door. It was slightly ajar. There was no point hanging about. I went in, replaced the door as it was, and crept up the steps to the top. That was the worst bit of all. I couldn't hear a thing—for all I knew, Harris might be just beyond the door at the top. I had to risk it. I came to the last door, peeped inside, found all quiet, and went through. I didn't waste any time, I went up the staircase to the tower and shut myself up there, on the roof. That was bad, too. At any moment I thought—"

But Simon had listened long enough.

"Yeah, we get the gist," he said. "Harris didn't come up. You were left safe inside with all your stuff."

"That's about the size of it," Marcus admitted.

He stopped talking. Simon nodded slowly and reached out to pry another biscuit from the packet. Emily sat slumped on the chair, looking miserably at Marcus. She knew very well she had to act, but she was now weighted down both by anxiety and by a guilt that had been growing throughout the telling of his story, and this made her feel helpless, panicky, and rather nauseous all at the same time.

However, she did her best.

"Marcus," she said, "it's brilliant that you managed to get here, and you've done really well getting all the equipment and everything. I'm sure you'll be able to avoid Harris as long as you like. But sooner or later you are going to have to leave the castle and sort things out another way."

She was watching him closely. His lip curled as she said this.

"What your dad did was wrong," she went on hurriedly, "and you were right to get out. But you shouldn't coop yourself up like this, as if you were on the run."

"I'm not on the run," Marcus interrupted. "I'm retreating to a position I can defend. And there's no other option."

"But there is," Emily said. "Go to the police. Parents aren't allowed to hit their kids. It's illegal."

"I'm not going to the police, Em. They wouldn't be interested."

"Of course they would. They'd sort it out for you, wouldn't they, Simon?" Come on, she thought, back me up here.

"I dunno." He was picking at his fingernails, studiously disinterested.

"I'm telling you, Marcus, they could have your dad up for it."

He laughed harshly. "Think they'd believe me? You're mad!"

"Look at your bloody face, for heaven's sake! Of course they'd believe you."

"So what if they did? Let's say they put Dad away. Great! I'd be allowed to swan off home on my own then, would I? 'The house is yours, now, sir.' I don't think so."

"This must happen all the time! There'd be ways—"

"Too right there would. And where d'you think I'd end up?"

"Well, where are you ending up now? Freezing your arse off here!"

Simon looked up suddenly. "You shouldn't count on the police, Em," he said. "It would be Marcus's word against his dad's when it came down to it. They'd look at his dad, see he's got a good job and that, then look at Marcus. . . . Well . . ."

"Yeah?" Emily retorted. "Why wouldn't they believe Marcus?"

Simon's lips thinned. "'Nice clothes you've got there, son. New, are they? Bought them with your own money, did you? Right, right. You must have a decent part-time job, then. What d'you earn?' You don't know them, Em. They'd look at Marcus and see a thief."

Marcus listened, white-faced.

"I'm not going to the police," he said.

"Yeah, police aren't the answer," Simon said. "Don't know what is, though."

Emily snorted. "Exactly," she said. "You haven't got a

clue. All that's rubbish, Marcus. Don't listen to him."

"I know more about it than you," Simon countered. "There is one thing I do agree with Em about, though—you shouldn't stay here. You'll get pneumonia."

"Well, where else am I going to go?"

Simon shrugged. "Dunno. You got any relations?"

"Oh, sure." Marcus put on a falsetto voice. "'Poor Nick, it's been so hard for him. Be a good boy for Nick, won't you. . . .' You must be *kidding*. They love him."

"Mmm. Dunno, then. It's tricky. Any more ideas, Em?"

Emily gave him a look. There was a silence. All three sat staring into different corners of the hut, listening to the humming of the heater. Finally Marcus roused himself to action.

"Well," he said. "I'm here for the moment, and I haven't been wasting my time, either. I've got to show you something I've discovered. It's brilliant. Come on!"

He got up with an energy that neither Emily nor Simon shared, and opened the hut door. An icy blast swept into the warm interior, routing them out to stumble after him across the courtyard to an arch that Emily had not previously explored. It led on to a broad circular stairwell, which Marcus scaled two steps at a time, the others traipsing after. On the next landing was the room with the door that led to the entrance stairs. It was still hanging open from when Emily had dashed through it.

"This has got a latch," Marcus said, pointing it out, "but there's no way to secure it. No lock. Now, this *next* one . . ." He headed down the long flight of steps to the second door halfway along. It too was open. Marcus pushed it so that the latch clicked shut. "Look at this."

He indicated two deep rectangular grooves in the stonework of the arch, halfway up the door on either side. They were the same shape as letter boxes, only a little bigger and turned ninety degrees so that they ran straight up and down.

"What do you think these are?" he asked.

Emily shook her head, but Simon's eyes brightened.

"I know," he said. "It's for a bar of some kind. To keep the door shut."

Marcus nodded excitedly. "Exactly! It's for a draw-bar. You slot a thick plank of wood in here and it prevents the door from being opened from the outside. It would need a battering ram to break it down."

"So?" Emily was unimpressed.

"Don't you see? This is the one weak spot of the castle, as far as I'm concerned. Harris or anyone else with a key can just open the door down there and waltz right in. But with a drawbar inserted here I could stop them from getting into the keep. They'd be stuck on the staircase."

"Under the murder-holes," Simon said. A grin widened slowly on his face.

"That's it. Anyway, it won't come to that if I can keep out of sight. But if there is any trouble, I've got a drawbar ready-made."

"Where from?"

"From the hut. It's made of planks of just the right width. I've checked—they'd fit. And a couple of them at the back are loose. I could rip them out if I had to."

"If you had tools."

"I do. I pinched a few of Dad's things. Hammer, Stanley knife, things like that."

Simon whistled. "Good job."

"I'm out of here," Emily said suddenly. "You can stay if you want, Simon." She turned and set off up the stairs.

"Where are you going, Em?" Marcus said, following her. "I've got a couple of other things to show you."

"I'm not interested. I've had enough."

"Em—"

"Sorry, Marcus. You can stay here as long as you want. It's up to you."

She reemerged in the entrance lobby, Marcus and Simon hard on her heels.

"It's all right, you don't have to follow me," she said tartly. "I can walk to the rope on my own. You carry on playing your games. It'll be great fun for you, but I want to get back to the real world, if you don't mind."

Marcus shrugged. "Do what you like." He hopped onto the low deep sill beneath one of the room's narrow window slits. "I'll be fine."

Emily looked at Simon. "What about you?"

He stood silent, undecided. Emily turned to go. "Whatever. I'll see you."

As she turned, Marcus made a strange choking sound. He staggered backward off the sill, his legs collapsing under him as he landed on the floor. His mouth gaped. To Emily's horror he began to moan in a continuous high whine that raised the hackles on the back of her neck.

First Emily and then Simon rushed over and knelt down at his side.

"Marcus, what is it?"

"Are you all right?"

"What's happened? What's the matter?"

"Some sort of fit—"

"Do you need a doctor? Simon, he's gone all pale."

Marcus's whine broke off into a stuttering cough.

His eyes, which had been staring straight ahead, began to turn wildly in all directions. His mouth closed, then opened again; he seemed to be trying to speak.

"What is it, mate?"

"Can you sit up properly? Let's get him up onto the windowsill, we could get his back against—"

At this suggestion Marcus's choking broke out anew. He shook his head frenziedly from side to side.

"No, no—outside . . ."

"What? What's outside?"

"Did you see something?"

"What's outside, mate?"

Marcus's eyes finally met theirs; he looked from one to the other and back again, then swallowed and spoke.

"Don't go near the window . . . he might see you."

"Who might? Who's out there?"

"I saw him, down by the moat, looking up at the keep. He may have seen me!"

"Who? Who did you see?"

Marcus took a deep breath, then spoke in a voice that was barely a whisper.

"My dad."

12

For a moment Emily and Simon could only stare speechlessly at Marcus. Then Simon straightened his back.

"Your *dad's* out there?" he said incredulously. "Your dad? Give over!"

"He is! Don't go near the window! Don't, Simon!"

"Oh, I'll be careful, don't worry. No one's going to see anything. . . ." Keeping his back to the stonework, he climbed onto the windowsill and, edging nearer to the slit of light, peered out.

"There *is* someone down there, you know," he said. "Bloke standing in the shadow of the arch. Hard to make him out. What makes you think it's your dad, Marcus?"

"Because I know my dad when I see him! Oh, God, how did he find me?"

"Come and look again. You need to make sure."

"No way. He'll see me."

"Marcus, this is a bloody arrow slit, and we're ten meters up. If you don't stick your nose out the crack, there's no way he'll spot you. I want you to look again and confirm it's your dad, because it doesn't seem likely to me that he's managed to track you down, unless you told him where you've been the last few days."

"Of course I didn't! But it's him—"

"Well, come and look, then!" Simon snarled.

Almost like a sleepwalker, Marcus struggled to his feet and approached the window. Simon drew back and gave him space to pass along the edge of the deep windowsill toward the strip of light. He peered once, then jerked back with a yelp.

"It's him?" Emily asked.

Marcus nodded dumbly. Simon shook his head.

"How the hell—? It doesn't make sense. Shift out the way. I want to see what he does."

He resumed his spying position, while Marcus dropped to the floor again beside Emily.

"He's going to come in and get me," he said in a small voice.

Emily reached out and held his hand. "Of course he won't." She was trying for a sensible, matter-of-fact sort of voice, but it came out high and squeaky. "He hasn't got a key, has he?"

"Harris may have given him one."

"Oh, talk sense! Of course he hasn't. Harris would be here, otherwise. In fact," she went on, warming to her reassuring theme, "I don't believe he can know you're here. He's guessing. If we keep still he'll go away."

"What car's your dad got?" Simon put in suddenly.

"Ford Fiesta. Blue."

"It *is* him then; I can see it in the car park."

"What's he doing?" Emily asked. "Just looking?"

"Yeah. He's kind of hanging around. He's edgy. Keeps looking over his shoulder. Like he's the one on the run."

"Well, the place *is* closed," Emily said. "He shouldn't be here either, should he?"

Simon nodded. "These things must run in the family. *Hold on*—he's moving!"

"Oh, God!" Marcus scratched distractedly at his hair. "Where's he going?"

"He's coming this way."

"Oh, God!"

"Don't worry—he can't get in. Em—the rope's hidden, isn't it?"

"Yep."

"Okay. We're safe, then. He's going round the tower. He'll be looking for the door. Come on." Simon leaped from the windowsill and darted toward the passage.

Marcus cried out in agitation. "Wait! Where are you going?"

"I want to see what he does. Follow me, but *quietly*."

One after the other they ran down the passageway toward the pillared room, Marcus instinctively ducking every time he passed by a window or arrow slit. As he entered the room, Simon slowed to a stealthy creep, each step an exaggerated tiptoe in his bulky boots. The others followed suit, advancing in single file toward the deep arched window that looked out over the wintry fields.

They hadn't quite reached it when they heard footsteps scuffling directly below. As they stood stock-still, a creak and muffled rattle sounded, coming both from the window and up through the murder-holes. Pressure was being applied to the keep's great door. Simon gave a sign for utter silence, while Marcus bit his lip till it turned white. The rattling came again, twice more, then it broke off. Emily thought she heard a muttered curse drift up through the window as the scuffling in the melting snow resumed outside. Simon indicated the others should lean in close.

"He's going to go around the keep," he hissed. "Looking for another way in. He must be so sure you're in here, Marcus."

"But how?" Emily hissed back. "If you didn't tell

him where you've been going, how could he possibly—"

Her voice trailed away. She was watching Marcus's face as she spoke and observed a queasy mixture of horror and realization dawning. He looked very green.

Simon raised his eyebrows. "So," he said. "What did you do?"

Marcus's voice was dull, drained of all hope. "It was that pamphlet. You know, the one with the map of the castle in it. I took it home to read last time, and I don't remember packing it. . . . It must have slipped down the side of the bed or something, so I missed it when I left. And Dad must have found it. . . ."

He put his head in his hands and groaned.

"Keep it down," Simon snapped.

Marcus groaned silently.

"You *are* an idiot, Marcus," Emily whispered. "All that preparation and you leave a clue signposting the way to your hideout. Now what are we going to do?"

Simon patted Marcus's shoulder. "It'll still be all right," he said. "Your dad can't get in, so he'll think you can't, either. So what if you've been hanging out here recently? There's no reason for him to think you'll be shacked up in the castle now."

Marcus nodded weakly. "I suppose you're right."

"Of course I am. The first thing is to see him off. He

won't hang about; the wind's picking up again. Let's go back to the other side and keep watch."

They trooped back to the entrance lobby and stationed themselves at the window, Simon standing, the other two crouching on the sill. Looking out, Emily could see the nearby gatehouse, several chunks of ruined wall, the great shadowy depression of the moat and, far off over the field, the boundary hedge. Beyond was the car park. A single blue car was parked there, its tracks slewing visibly across the icy slush. They waited awhile in silence.

At length Simon nodded his head slightly. Marcus stiffened. Emily craned her neck forward and looked. A man walked into view, heading for the gatehouse. He had his back to them. He wore a dark green fleece and black jeans and had a red woolen hat pulled down low over his head. The man picked his way slowly toward the moat, slipping once or twice on the uneven ground. Presently he passed under the gatehouse arch, crossed the bridge, and moved away across the field toward the gate in the hedge. They watched him go. It wasn't until he reached his car that he turned around and stared back at the castle, but he was then too far off for Emily to make out his face. He stood there for what seemed like an age, before finally opening the door and getting in.

Even now he was in no haste to leave. For several minutes more the car remained stationary, its occupant invisible behind the dull sheen of the windows.

Emily could hear Marcus pleading under his breath—"Why won't you go? Why won't you just *go*?"—and at last his prayers were answered by the distant growl of the engine starting.

The car drove away down the lane, into the woods and out of sight. Only then did the three of them relax. Emily's back ached with tension.

"Well," Simon said. "He's gone."

"Did you see him? Did you see his expression?" Marcus asked, his voice high-pitched with excitement. "He's furious! He's livid! He is *so* mad that he can't find me! Even when I leave him a clue, he can't track me down!"

"He made a pretty good stab at it," Emily said quietly.

"I'm safe in my castle! The defenses are holding fast. Did you see his face, Simon? He wanted to get me so badly. Did you see it?"

Simon frowned. "I might have . . . it was a bit far away."

"I couldn't see it," Emily said. "Anyway, that's not important. We need to decide what you're going to do now."

"Do? I'm staying here. It's all the better now he's looked round and seen how *impossible* it is for me to be here!" Marcus laughed to himself. "Listen, it's getting on a bit. I want to get myself sorted for the night. Could you give me a hand with the heater again, Simon? I need to get it upstairs."

"Up there again? You must be joking!"

"I'll make it worth your while—I'll show you some more of the defenses I've been planning. They're great!"

"Defenses first, heater after—*if* it's worth it."

"You're on. They're downstairs."

Marcus shot off down the stairwell, and Simon, with a shrug, began to follow him. As he disappeared around the bend in the stairs, he looked back at Emily, who hadn't moved a muscle. She shook her head at him.

"I'll be along in a minute," she said.

When she was alone, Emily stretched and sat herself more comfortably on the windowsill. Then she closed her eyes and tried to think in a clear and sensible manner. This was difficult. A host of conflicting thoughts were crashing around in her mind like a disorderly crowd, creating a hubbub that drowned out everything except her general agitation. It was very hard to make sense of it all and work out what to do.

She concentrated: Okay, number one thought. It was stupid for Marcus to continue hiding in the castle. That was clear. He would either die of exposure or get caught and be done for vandalism, trespassing, and the rest. So . . .

Thought number two was also straightforward, or seemed to be. Marcus was in danger from his dad. No doubt about it. If his word wasn't enough, you had his bruises to go on, and they spoke out loud and clear.

Not that you couldn't just accept his word, of course, but . . .

Emily sighed. The trouble with Marcus was that he talked too much for his own good. It was hard to keep track of what he said, hard to sift things so you saw them properly. Sometimes you couldn't be sure that he hadn't got a little carried away. But there was no mistaking what had happened to his face—and his dad *was* on his trail. Marcus was in real trouble; that was obvious enough.

So what to do? It got tricky here, because tainting everything in Emily's mind, sending everything off course, was the guilt that lay over her like a smothering cloud. She recognized it fully now. It was her fault that all of this had happened, her fault that they had returned to the castle and stayed out overnight, her fault that Marcus had been late back so that his dad had hit him. It was true that she wasn't to blame for him being late, precisely, but it didn't feel far off. And if she hadn't inspired them to stay over, to treat the castle like a home, Marcus wouldn't have bolted back here now when he was in need.

Or would he? It was hard to know. Sometimes Marcus seemed happy to ignore things the way they were and just follow whatever fancy took him. Like all this rubbish about defending the castle. Simon was too easily impressed by that; any talk of tools and traps and defenses and he was putty in Marcus's hands.

So what should they do? Going to the police still seemed the only sensible idea any of them had had, but Marcus had rejected it out of hand. That was Simon's fault—if he wasn't so hung up on the police he might have seen the sense in it. No, neither of them would ever agree to that plan, and she couldn't go to the police on her own.

Could she?

Emily opened her eyes and looked around. A distant, muffled bang came from the direction of the hall. She winced. Best ignore it.

The police . . . After all, she *could* contact them, ring them up . . . It would be easy enough that evening. Maybe she could do it anonymously, not give her name, just ring off when she'd told them about the castle. . . . No—Marcus would tell them about her, that was no good.

Or she could just tell it to them straight, no lies, no fudging. They'd cut right to the heart of the matter (Marcus's dad) and overlook the other stuff, their trespassing, the damage done to ancient monuments, all that.

Emily told herself that this was so, but she still felt sick inside.

Also, if she went to the police, Marcus and Simon would regard it as the blackest treachery. They would never speak to her again.

She groaned softly under her breath. All this heavy thinking and she was still coming back to her original position. Do nothing for the moment. All being well, Marcus would get so bored and cold after a day or two that he would listen to her about the police. Then they could leave the castle out of the story all together.

With this reluctant conclusion fresh in her mind, Emily looked up to see Simon emerging from the stairs. He was red in the face and puffing, and carried a long, horizontal plank of wood, on which was balanced a pile of small rocks and pieces of stone. Emily's heart sank to a new low.

"What," she said icily, "have you got there?"

Simon spoke with wheezing enthusiasm: "It's the pla—the drawbar for the door down there. We're going to test it. We got it from the hut like Marcus said. He's got some brilliant tools; cut through wood like cheese."

"And the rocks?"

"Ammunition. Hold on, I've got to get rid of them or I'll drop."

He advanced slowly to the passageway that led to the pillared room, only to find that the corridor was too narrow for the plank. With a sigh he shuffled himself around to face the wall, and with some difficulty began to proceed sideways up the passage like a crab. Emily, stony-faced, watched him go. A little later she heard a crash and a cry of pain. Her expression did not change. After a discreet pause Simon reappeared, still holding the plank and limping badly.

"Nearly made it to the murder-holes before my hand slipped," he said, massaging his left ankle. "Ow." He glanced up at her. "I said *Ow*. It's quite sore."

"So the rocks are going to be chucked through the murder-holes if the castle is attacked?" Emily asked, ignoring his plaintive sighs. "You'll do that yourself, will you? Honestly, Simon, you are such a—"

"Someone drop something?" A cheerful voice sounded behind her. Marcus was also bearing a small arsenal of stones, this time contained in his rucksack. "These beauties should do the job, eh?" He grinned and swung the rucksack off his back onto the floor. "Ah, that's better! I'll shift them across properly later. Let's try the bar, Simon."

"Hold on." Once again, Emily felt as if she were losing her bearings. She tried to reestablish some order in the world. "Guys, I've got to go. I need to be home for tea, and it's past four. I have to help Mum with stuff."

They looked at her blankly. Even to her own ears, her excuse seemed strangely insubstantial—not just untrue, but inherently odd, peculiar. "And it's getting dark," she added. "Won't be able to get down the wall soon. Don't you think, Simon?"

"I suppose."

"I'll need your help to get down. Look, Marcus, we'll come back and see you tomorrow. Check that all's well. That's okay by you, isn't it?"

"I don't know, Em." He looked at her apologetically. "It depends."

"On what?"

"On what the situation is. If all's clear I can let you up. Otherwise, I won't be chucking the rope down, will I?"

Emily heard herself laugh mirthlessly. "Oh, come on, nothing's going to happen."

"Nothing's going to happen *tonight*," Marcus corrected her. "They won't come in the dark, unless they're stupid. But tomorrow . . . I'm not sure. I've got to be prepared."

"Okay, then. Fine." She wanted to get out. "We'll see you then."

"Hold on, we need to organize it. I'm not going to be hanging around on the walkway all day for you. I'll spend most of my time in the window here, watching the gate. That's where the attack'll come from."

"So let's arrange a time, then," Emily said, impatiently. She felt the ground shifting again under her feet.

"Early," Marcus said. He thought for a moment. "Best thing is to synchronize our watches. I make it 4:06 now. Let's say ten o'clock tomorrow. I'll be waiting for you then with the rope. Don't be late or you won't get in."

"Ten it is." Simon seemed happy with the arrangement. "You'll manage the plank okay, will you?"

"I can test that now, no worries. There is one thing, though. Could you bring some bottles of water with you when you come? I haven't brought enough and the well's dry, of course."

By now Emily was at the arch leading to the walkway. Her head was spinning. She urgently needed to leave the castle right away, to be alone. Maybe solitude and open air would help clear her mind. She gave Marcus a long, last, withering look and went through the arch with Simon at her heels.

"Don't forget the water!" Marcus called after them. "And thanks for coming—it's great to have reinforcements!"

13

In the middle of the night, the weather turned again. Emily was woken at 3:30 A.M. by a gust of wind that struck her bedroom window with the vicious impact of a slamming door. The wind screamed up and away across her roof, and Emily, muddled with sleep, leaned over and pushed the heavy curtain aside. Even through the double-glazing, the coldness of the night tickled her flesh. The streetlight across the road showed up as a dull fuzz of orange, a whirling tumult. Snow shards hit the pane and built up on the sill outside. Below the streetlight, the paving slabs that the man opposite had painstakingly scraped clear had vanished again under a thick cloak. As she watched, the outer glass shuddered with another blow. Emily let the curtain drop and fell back against her pillow.

"You *idiot*, Marcus," she said.

★ ★ ★

The blizzard was still continuing at breakfast. Emily put on several extra layers and surreptitiously brought her boots to lurk near the back door. Permission for going out in such conditions would not be easily granted and was better avoided altogether. She loitered, taking frequent anxious glances at her watch, until her parents settled down to unknown chores and the coast was clear. Emily grabbed two thick coats, shoved on her boots, and slipped out into the snow.

At the edge of the woods the snow was falling so thickly that Emily almost missed Simon. He was standing motionless against a tree, gazing out into the swirling whiteness. As she approached, stumbling over the hidden brambles, he turned to her abruptly.

"Did you get the water?"

"Oh, no, I forgot. Tough. But Marcus isn't going to want it now, surely."

"I brought some—a couple of bottles. Did you see the police?"

"What?" That dizzy sick feeling again.

"There's a patrol car in the village. I came out of the shop and nearly bumped into two coppers going in."

"What did they want?"

"I didn't hang around to find out, did I? Use your head. Maybe they're on Marcus's trail. Working with his dad. I *told* you they weren't to be trusted."

"Simon, we've got to get him out of that castle. If they find him there, we're all busted."

"It's the safest place for him at the moment, with the village on the lookout."

"This is all wrong, Simon."

"We can discuss it in the warm. It's five to ten."

He began walking down the slope to the humped outline of the boundary fence. Emily followed, lifting her legs as high as she could to clear the buried thorns. The snow was falling so thickly now that she could only squint, and her view was restricted to three or four meters all around. With some difficulty they located the gap in the hedge—the strips of wire showing clean and black in the swirling white. Then over the field, through snowdrifts that were deeper than ever, to a bridge that had almost vanished. Its planks were smothered, its edges invisible as they crossed it. Emily imagined straying to the left or right, somehow missing the safety rails and falling away into the blankness. The snow would deaden the sound, her crumpled body would be a spot of color quickly covered up. . . . She realized she was dawdling; Simon's shape was drawing away.

She extended her stride, under the gatehouse and onward, until the great, gray bulk of the castle, invisible in detail, began to swallow up her field of vision. As she drew closer, she made out the nearby towers and battlements, a few windows and arrow slits showing through like smudged pencil strokes. The familiar imperfections—the ruined corner of the tower, the cracks in the walls, the crumbling stonework—could not be seen. For all the world, the keep looked whole and strong.

They stumbled around to the far side, gauging the position of their entrance as well as they could. Simon looked at his watch, then up at the wall. The wind buffeted their hoods; snowflakes stippled their faces.

"He should be there." Simon leaned close to Emily. "We're only three minutes late."

"Can he see us? I can barely see the hole."

Simon gave a piercing whistle that was carried off by the air. He tried shouting Marcus's name. No face appeared, no rope came down. Emily called, too.

"Having told us to synchronize watches, he's probably lost his," Simon grunted. "What do you think? Should we bang on the door?"

"We'd just get stones thrown at us—hang on, there he is!"

A distant blotch of orange and blue appeared above. Simon and Emily gesticulated and called. The blotch considered them, then retreated. A moment later, the rope tumbled down in front of them. First Emily and then Simon scaled the wall, their feet slipping on the frosty stones.

Marcus was waiting at the top, cowled by his all-weather hood. Snow danced behind him in the empty hall. Without a word he beckoned them along the passage, out of the worst of the weather. Emily expected him to climb the stairs to their room, but instead he vanished into the chapel, leading them around the castle and back to the entrance lobby, where the window overlooked the car park and the gate.

Once there, Marcus removed his hood.

"Have you got the water?"

He had big bags under his eyes, and his face looked pinched and cold. Emily thought his hand shook as he reached out to take the bottles from Simon's rucksack.

"Is that all?" Marcus said. "Two bottles?"

"Em forgot hers."

"Bloody typical. You ask for supplies and they don't get through."

"Get stuffed," Emily said. "You're not going to drink all that, so don't pretend you are."

"Drink it? No, thanks!" Marcus leaped onto the windowsill and peered out into the raging snow. "I've got a bottle of Coke upstairs. This is for my defenses. Anyway, it doesn't matter—I've got my camping stove. I can melt snow. It just takes longer that way."

"What defenses?" Simon asked. "You didn't mention these yesterday."

"Tricks and traps, mate, tricks and traps. I'll show you."

Taking up one of the bottles, he led them through the arch to the walkway that ran alongside the vanished hall. He stopped next to one of the arches that gave way to the empty space. Whirling flakes filled the air and the walkway was flecked with settling snow. Marcus bent down and unscrewed the bottle top.

"Right," he said, grinning up at them. "Watch this. Don't get wet!"

So saying, he tipped the bottle up and gently poured the water out, moving his hand in a broad circle so that almost the whole width of the passage was covered in a thin puddle.

"Great," Marcus said as he stood up, "I only used half the bottle. This'll do for another on the next side round. Do you see?" he went on. "The stone's worn down here, so it's collecting nicely. Give it half an hour and it'll be an ice trap."

"Yes," Emily said. "I see."

"I'm going to booby-trap all the walkways, especially near these arches. It might save me if the enemy breaks in. *I'll* know where to jump, but they won't. With any luck—"

"—they'll slip and fall," Emily interrupted. "I know."

"Clever," Simon said.

With this, they trooped back to the entrance room. Marcus was anxious not to be away from the window for too long. He sat on the sill, from where he had a good view out at the snow, and gestured at the plank leaning against the wall nearby.

"Should work perfectly," he said airily. "Fits as snug as a bug in those slots."

Emily drew a deep breath. She would make one final attempt, then she would go. "Look, Marcus," she began, "we've all had a great time here, and your defenses are superb, second to none. But take it from me, there's nowhere else to go with it. You look knackered, you look ill. You can't stay here. We need to decide on a different plan."

Marcus bristled. "What are you talking about? I feel great! Never better!" And it was true that he seemed possessed by a dynamic energy—his movements were quick, decisive as a bird's, and his eyes had the brightness of fever. "I had a wonderful night here all on my own. Never felt such comfort. The room was hot, I ate a meal fit for a lord, I walked round the hall in the middle of a storm. And you're trying to tell me that isn't how to live!"

"It's fine—for a night. But you can't stay here forever."

He glanced out; the blizzard was lessening a little. "No," he said. "Only while I'm threatened."

"The threat's not going to go away, Marcus! Sooner or later—"

"Oh, shut up, Em. You're repeating yourself."

Emily boiled with frustration. "Am I? Right, I'll shut up. And if you get caught in here, as you undoubtedly will, then we'll all suffer, all three of us. But you're fine with that, aren't you? Your problem, Marcus, is that you're totally selfish!"

She hadn't meant to lose her temper, but having done so she found she didn't care. She relished Marcus's outrage, the fury in his voice.

"Oh, that's it, is it?" he cried. "You claim to be anxious about me, but really you're just worried about getting into trouble yourself! Don't worry, I won't snitch on you, Em. You just go away and keep your head down."

"Don't twist my words!"

"Um, guys . . ."

"The fact is I'm *untwisting* them, that's what you don't like!"

"Guys . . ."

"*What*, Simon?"

"We have company. . . ."

As one, their heads turned. Out beyond the field a car was driving slowly along the lane. They could not hear its engine; all sounds were deadened in the new white world. The snow still descended, but more gently than before. Now and again small flurries were whipped up, billowed and discarded by the wind. In silence, the car rolled into the car park, plowing through the powder, and drew to a halt in the farthest corner. It was a small model, colored brown, although its roof and bonnet still had a thick white coating. The taillights remained on. No one got out.

"Come on, then," Marcus breathed finally. "*Do* something."

"Like drive off," Simon said.

"Why don't they get out?" Emily asked.

"It's some sightseer, maybe. Some tourist."

"In this weather?"

"Looks like he's got his engine running. He'll be off soon."

"Either that or he's just keeping himself warm."

"But why is he waiting?"

"One thing," Simon said suddenly. "He's local."

"Why?"

"He wouldn't have all the snow on the car roof else. Would he?—it'd have fallen off."

They digested this in silence, watching the distant car through the falling snow. Nothing happened. Emily felt her toes growing numb through her boots and double layers of sock; she began to grow restless. Simon started fidgeting too, and at last even Marcus rubbed his neck with a gloved hand and pulled his eyes away.

"Well," he said, "they don't seem to be doing anything, whoever they—ah, shit."

Another car was moving along the lane. This one had no covering of snow. It was blue and very familiar—they had seen it the day before.

"Your dad's persistent, isn't he?" Simon said.

The new car entered the car park with agonizing deliberation and pulled over alongside the brown one. Its lights went off, the door opened, and a figure in a green fleece emerged. Emily sensed Marcus shudder slightly. As his father approached the other car, its driver's door opened and a man got out. All three watchers in the castle caught their breath.

"Oh, God," Marcus said. "That's Harris, isn't it?"

"They're coming to look round," Emily said. "We've got to get out right now."

Marcus and Simon said nothing.

"Don't you understand, you fools? If we go now, they won't find us."

But they were mesmerized, their mouths open. Emily looked out again. The two figures in the car park were staring back down the lane at—

Emily gave a small whimper. A third vehicle was

negotiating the entrance to the car park with rather more speed and panache than the previous two. It skidded to a halt at a dramatic diagonal. Even from a distance, Emily could make out the yellow-and-black markings, the little light on the roof. After a brief pause, the doors opened and two policemen got out. Marcus's father and Harris trudged over to greet them.

"That's all we need," Simon said through his teeth. "The bloody police."

Marcus got abruptly to his feet. "The bar! The drawbar—I've got to put the bar in position!" His eyes were wide, and he did not quite seem to be addressing them. Seizing the plank, he struggled with it to the main door and disappeared down the steps, his voice echoing back: "Keep watch! Don't take your eyes off them!"

Emily turned to Simon, who was gazing out of the window. "We've got to convince him!" she cried. "He's going to do something stupid."

"Mmm?" Simon had a far-off look in his eye. "Sorry, missed that."

"You've got to help me convince him to go!"

"Yes, but, Em, where *is* he going to go?"

"I don't know, but it's madness—"

Marcus tumbled back into the room, panting with exertion. "I don't think it'll be enough!" he exclaimed.

"I should have done another plank, doubled the thickness. They might be able to break through that one."

"Quit worrying," Simon said. "It'll hold."

"I hope so. Oh, God, look, they're coming."

Far off, at the boundary of the castle grounds, Harris was unlocking the gate. As they watched, he pushed it open and stood aside to allow the others to pass through.

Emily took hold of Marcus's shoulder and swung him bodily around. "Right," she said, speaking as calmly as she could. "This is your last chance. We've got maybe five minutes before they get here. If we slip out the back now, they won't have a hope of catching us. If we stay, we're cooped up for good. Do you understand?"

Marcus frowned. "Ow, you're hurting me."

"That's nothing to what your dad's going to do when he gets here. Let's go!" The urgency in her voice seemed to affect Marcus. He was wavering; she saw doubt in his face. "Come on!" she insisted. She was almost dragging him bodily toward the passage.

"Wait," he said. "What about my stuff?"

"We haven't time for that! Leave it!" She pulled again, but something in Marcus had snapped back into position. He wrenched her hand free. "No," he said quietly. "That's my stuff you're talking about. I've worked hard to bring it here. I'm not just going to leave it to the enemy." He stepped back from her. "This is my castle. I'm not running away. They won't be able to get in."

"Ah!" Emily cried out with frustration. "Simon— help me!"

He didn't meet her eyes, but looked down at the floor. The action reminded her of their first meeting. "I don't know, Em, I think Marcus is right. They won't be able to get in."

"What about the police?"

"They won't be able to get in, either. That'll be worth seeing." Simon smiled a little.

"But then—"

"They're on the bridge," Marcus said.

"—we'll be trapped." She felt helpless, carried along between the stubbornness of one and the defiance of the other. "All right," she said. "You two stay. I'm going."

"What?" Marcus spun around, his eyes round with shock. "Em—you can't! You can't leave me now, not when the enemy's actually attacking! That would be terrible, that would be betrayal!"

"It would be common sense!"

"They're through the gatehouse and heading for the front door," Simon said.

"We've got to get to our positions!" Marcus left the

window. "Em, you do what you like. Go if you want. No one will see. It's up to you."

He vanished into the passage that led to the pillared room. With only the briefest pause, Simon followed him. Emily was left standing, miserable and alone. She imagined shinning down the rope and running off to safety, hiding in the trees, walking back to her parents' house. They would probably be watching television or making lunch. She looked at her watch. Only 11:20— early yet, earlier than she'd thought. A mumble of voices rose from beyond the window: the enemy was here.

She imagined sliding down the rope, running with seven-league strides that ate up the ground. Running for safety while the enemy was at the door.

Her room waited for her, with its bed, bookshelf, plywood desk, her old array of teddy bears, its radiator. Here in the castle, the wind whistled through the gaping arches, and flecks of snow landed on the flagstones. Her fingers were numb inside her gloves. She thought of warmth, comfort, and betrayal.

She should leave at once, but she could not bring herself to do so. The images of her room were weak and unfulfilling; they faded, and the castle's solid strength remained. She could not hide while the others stayed— like it or not, she had been instrumental in bringing them here, and she could not desert them now.

Emily was awash with fear and with a loyalty that was almost inseparable from guilt. She felt very sick.

When the wave of nausea had ebbed, she adjusted her hat so that her ears were properly covered. Then, with a deep breath, she set off down the passage to the pillared room.

Marcus and Simon were squatting in the middle of the floor, each crouched over a murder-hole, each with his own pile of rocks and stones. They did not look up as she entered. Through a window came the sound of crunching snow, coughs, muttered voices. A rattling noise followed, and with it the barely audible rasp of Harris's voice.

"Be patient. The lock's stiff." More rattling. "It freezes up in these conditions."

Emily went to crouch beside Marcus. The rattling ended with the protesting shriek of ancient hinges moving. There was a slight creaking as the door swung open, the sound carrying more strongly through the murder-hole than through the window.

Marcus was staring intently down the hole, blocking it so that Emily could not see clearly into the passage below. He picked up a large lump of rock. Out of the corner of her eye, Emily saw Simon do the same.

Footsteps sounded in the passage below, drawing nearer.

A voice came drifting up; Harris's again. "This is a fool's errand."

Another voice, peaceable, relaxed. "Just routine checking, sir."

Harris grunted. "You've seen yourself the door was locked."

Marcus tensed; he lifted the rock over the center of the hole, holding it loosely between finger and thumb. Emily cupped her mouth in both hands and leaned close to Marcus's ear. "If you do that," she breathed, "they'll never believe you about your dad. Then he'll have won."

Marcus gave no sign that he had heard. His hand hovered over the hole, shaking a little. The footsteps came closer. Marcus's hand quivered. Now the steps were right underneath. They passed on up the flight of stairs and Marcus was still holding the rock. He let his hand fall to the floor and sunk his head down against his knee.

Simon looked over from his murder-hole and, shrugging, put his rock down.

A muttered exclamation of surprise came from below, followed by repeated heavy thuds. Marcus raised his head and smiled thinly.

Voices from up the passage: "What's wrong?" "Haven't you a key?"

Harris (perplexed, off guard): "I don't need one. This door's always open."

Another voice (irritable): "Well, it isn't now. Let me try." (More thudding, expressions of effort and annoyance.)

The peaceable voice again: "Something's blocking it. Can anything have fallen against the door on the other side?"

Harris (whining, aggrieved): "No, there's nothing . . . It's just stairs, just empty."

Peaceable voice: "Then someone's done it deliberately. Try again, Jones." (A particularly loud thud, a volley of swearing.) "No need for that sort of language, Jones. All right, we can't get in here. Any other way?"

Harris (indignant): "No."

Peaceable voice: "Interesting. Mind if we have a scout round outside, Mr. Harris?"

No answer came, but Harris had presumably given his assent, because the footsteps resumed, returning in the direction they had come. Simon looked across at Marcus expectantly, and Marcus lifted his hand again. Emily leaned closer to him.

"*Don't*, Marcus!" she hissed.

The footsteps stopped abruptly.

"I heard someone!" a new voice said from below. "Look! Those holes! Someone's up there!"

Emily, Marcus, and Simon froze.

"Yes," the peaceable voice said. "I heard it too." A single set of footsteps sounded on the stone floor below. Emily imagined the man peering up.

"That means there's more than one," the irritable voice said.

The footsteps were directly underneath them now. Simon shrank back from the lip of his hole. It's all right, Emily thought. You can't be seen.

A sudden beam of light speared up through Simon's murder-hole, cutting through the gray gloom and jabbing into the ceiling. Startled, Simon jerked backward and knocked into his pile of pebbles, which collapsed with a small but sustained clattering.

The beam of light vanished. Simon's face was chalky in the shadows.

Then the peaceable voice called up from below. "Hello? Hello?" It waited for a moment. "We know you're up there, son. Why don't you come down and let us in?"

Not a sound issued from any of the three; they didn't look at each other.

"Have you got a friend with you?" The voice

paused, then went on slowly, weighing each word carefully, judiciously. "Well, Marcus, I hope you can hear me. This is the police. There's no problem. We've got your dad here, son. He's anxious to see you. Why don't you come down and open the door? No one's angry, just anxious. Can you come and talk to us?"

The voice indeed seemed very reasonable and soothing, and Emily found that despite her fears about Marcus's father she rather agreed with what it said. It would be so much easier if they could just explain everything. She glanced across at Marcus and Simon in turn and saw self-doubt on both their faces. But no one said anything.

There was a sudden scuffle in the passageway below, and Harris's harsh, intemperate voice rang out. "Stop skulking up there and open this door! You're on private property—you know that? You're trespassing on the property of the heritage company, and if you've done the slightest bit of damage here you'll be prosecuted!"

The police officer began speaking to him hurriedly in undertones, but the damage had been done. The three listeners in the pillared room looked at one another aghast. From where she sat, Emily could see the plastic covers that Marcus had torn from the murderholes. Visions of courtrooms and judges swam hideously in her mind, and when the reasonable voice spoke again, its earlier inducements had been forgotten.

"Please don't be concerned, Marcus," it said. "I'm sure there won't be any trouble like that. We just want you to come down and open the door." A pause. "You don't *want* to get into any trouble, do you?" Emily could detect a hint of impatience in the voice. She shivered, but she saw Simon's face harden.

Then came the unexpected. "Oh, your dad wants a word," the voice said. "Here he is."

To Emily he did not *sound* like a vicious child beater—a rather dull, anxious voice drifted pleading through the floor. "Marcus, it's me, your dad. I've been . . . I've been ever so worried about you. Come down and come home with me. We can sort this. I'm not angry with you, son, not angry at all. Not about the money or anything."

Emily watched Marcus's expression in the ensuing silence. No change.

"I know we've had some problems . . . and, and I'm willing to work them out with you. But you've got to talk to me; it's no good running off. . . ." The voice petered out uncertainly, then began again. "We can go somewhere nice," it went on, "to talk about things. Somewhere better than this drafty old place, eh, Marcus? Bit warmer, eh? We could stay at a guesthouse, like we used to, by the sea. Come on, son, how about it? We both need a break. What do you say?"

Marcus looked down through the hole, unblinking. A murmur of voices could be heard, a quiet discussion. Then the dull voice spoke up again, more imploringly than ever.

"*Please*, Marcus. I tell you we can sort it out—you and me. We need to work at things, I know; but if we do that, we can get there, we can make it just like it was."

To Emily's great shock, Marcus's eyes flashed, his lips drew back in a snarl, and bending his head to the murder-hole, he let out a shout that was almost a scream. "Liar! It'll *never* be like it was!"

The cry echoed despairingly around the pillared room. In the passage below, a stunned silence was followed by a roar of rage.

"Stop being such a spoiled little fool! *Get down here!*"

His face ashen, teeth bared, Marcus threw himself back and, scooping up a double handful of stones, half dropped, half flung them down the murder-hole. There was a tremendous clattering and a cry of pain. He just had time to scoop another handful before Emily launched herself upon him. The impact knocked him away from the hole, scattering stones in all directions. Together they tumbled for an instant, Marcus on his back, Emily on top—then he shoved her off him, crashing her hard against the base of a pillar. She gasped, let go her grip, and felt Marcus wrench himself back toward the hole. Even as he did so, she saw Simon out of the corner of her eye, sweeping a pile of stones over the edge of his hole and conjuring another rattling cascade, another outburst of cries and oaths.

Marcus caught up another large rock, but before hurling it he paused, squinting eagerly down his murder-hole. "They've gone," he panted. "We've driven them back."

Sure enough, there was no sound in the passage beneath, but from beyond the window came the sharp confusion of four men talking over one another excitedly. The words were unintelligible, but Emily had no difficulty interpreting their anger.

Within the castle there was silence for a time. Marcus still crouched by the murder-hole, looking down into it, his breathing gradually slowing. Simon sat back on his haunches, idly tossing a small pebble between his hands. Emily remained sprawled against the pillar. Waves of disbelief crashed over her; her head was spinning with the horror of what had happened and with the deeper horror that she was fully, fatally implicated in it.

Simon stood upright and headed for the window.

His movement roused Emily a little. "What—what have you done?" Her voice was tiny, cracked; a child's voice.

"Shut up. I want to hear what they're saying." Stepping over her, Simon approached the window, leaned on the deep, sloping sill, and cautiously peered out into the brightness of the day. He leaned a little farther, then ducked down suddenly.

"No good," he said. "They're not stupid—they've walked a little way off to talk. He's on his radio—that's a bad sign. Hold on . . . One's set off . . . Yeah, he's heading round the keep, checking it out. He's rubbing his arm; must be the one I got. Your dad looks rough, Marcus . . . Head's bleeding; not much but it's a direct hit. Well done. He's going off with Harris. For first aid probably—good, so they're out of action for the moment. Didn't get Harris. Other cop's staying here, still on the radio.

"And that's the story," he concluded, turning back into the room. "We're surrounded. Reinforcements will be on their way." He stepped back over Emily's feet. "Marcus, wake up!"

There was a glazed expression on Marcus's face; far from being overjoyed, the success of his trap seemed of little interest to him beside the terrible immensity of what he had just done. With white knuckles he still clutched the final rock, still gazed into the hole as if he expected to see his father there.

"You did it," Simon said, nudging him gently with his boot. "You struck a blow back. You should feel proud."

"You idiots!" Emily cried. "We're in for it now. What did you go and do that for?—they'll kill us when they get in."

"*If* they get in." Simon seemed unable to keep still, pacing to and fro between the pillars. "But it was worth it for Marcus to get a chance at his dad—did you hear him screaming up at Marcus, then? Like a bloody wild animal. Savage, he was, you could hear it. Too right Marcus should want to get a blow back."

"Whatever. How are we going to get out?"

"We can't—now. They'll keep watch on all sides, keep the place surrounded. No chance of escape for the moment. Eh, Marcus—what do you think?" Another nudge with the toe cap, and this time Marcus blinked and looked up. He seemed disoriented.

"I don't know . . . what should we do?"

"Easy," Simon said. "We have to hold the keep. I thought you of all people would know that, Marcus; it's what Baron Hugh would have done. We add another piece of wood to the door. We man the walkways. . . . How are they going to climb up, anyway? Shin up like we did? I don't think so, and there's ice all over the walls today, worse than that first time. We've got a bit of food, a bit of water, even got some heat, which is more than they have. Come on, where's the fight in you? We *won* the first round."

As he spoke, a little light came back into Marcus's eyes, but Emily shook her head.

"You're mad," she said. "You think we can hold them off? Half the police in Norfolk are probably on their way right now!"

"So what if they catch us?" Simon shrugged. "What can they do?"

"Only lock us up!"

Simon shrugged again. "Then let's make it count. Let's do more than just ponce about and get done for trespassing. Let's really give Harris something to remember us by."

"Simon, our only chance is to get out now, before the reinforcements come."

"Are you kidding? The visibility's fine now that the snow's stopping. They'll catch us before we make it to the woods."

"Yeah, but if we stay, they'll smash the door down and catch us, anyway. Running gives us a chance."

"What time is it?" Marcus said suddenly.

"Twenty-five to twelve," Simon answered.

"When's it get dark?"

"About four. Might be earlier today. Yes—that's it! Marcus has got it, Em! We have to hold out for another four hours, or less if it snows again. When the light goes, we'll slip out down the rope and away over the fields. You and me can circle round into the village from another direction, in case they watch the lane. Marcus has his flashlight—he can pick his way across country till he hits another road."

"What happens then?" Marcus asked.

"That's your problem. We'll get you out of here. After that, mate, you're on your own."

Simon made another sortie to the window. "Policeman's still there. He's looking chilly. So, are we agreed, then?"

Emily made a face. "Don't see that I've got much choice."

"Nope," Simon said, grinning. "Not unless you want to go out and give yourself up to that chilly policeman. Marcus?"

"Of course."

"Till dark it is, then. We'd better get to work."

14

The enemy circled the keep. From windows, arrow slits, latrine holes, and other vantage points on all four sides, the defenders cautiously observed their movements. To begin with, only one policeman negotiated the thick snow at the base of the walls. He went slowly, studying the stonework as he went, doubtless searching for an alternative entrance. His companion remained stationed by the main door, standing well back out of the range of potential missiles. Occasionally he spoke into his radio. After fifteen minutes another car pulled up in the car park and disgorged two other officers, a man and a woman. They joined the man with the radio, who seemed to be the one in charge, and after a brief consultation, set off singly around the perimeter of the castle. Four police officers meant four sides of the keep watched at all times: if the defenders *had* sought to escape now, they would quickly have been captured. But no such attempt was made.

Inside the castle there was much activity. Before doing anything else, Marcus, who was recovering some of his energy and determination, climbed to his base in the restored room and scoured his supplies. He reappeared with three cans of drink and several chocolate bars, two of which he thrust into Emily's lap.

"Go on," he said. "It's high-energy, good for warmth."

After glum contemplation, Emily ate one of the bars. The chocolate tasted like cardboard in her dry mouth, even when she washed it down with Coke.

Marcus then disappeared to reinforce his defenses. Before joining him, Simon tried to rouse Emily from her depression. She was still sitting in the pillared room, head resting back on one column, staring at the cracks in the wall.

"At least guard the entrance for us," he said. "Our trouble is going to be keeping a watch on every side. I think it's most likely they'll try this way again. Okay? Give us a shout if anything happens."

Without enthusiasm, Emily did as she was told, lurking in the shadows as far away from the window as possible without losing her view of the policeman. Every couple of minutes she looked at her watch, willing the hands to move at lightning speed toward the magic time of dusk. Instead they dawdled—twelve o'clock came and went with agonizing slowness, and Emily found herself gazing at the skies imploringly, praying for a resumption of the snowstorm.

Outside, the policeman loitered, rocking back and forward on his feet, clapping his hands before him and walking in ornate loops and circles in a vain attempt to get warm. Periodically, one of his colleagues came past to make contact. Emily strained to catch their words but could not do so. Whether by accident or design, they spoke just low enough to frustrate her. Once, the senior officer looked up directly at her window, and Emily ducked away, sure that he must have seen her. But if he did so he gave no sign. The window was high up, narrow, and deep set. Perhaps it was okay. After a moment's consideration, she pulled her hat down as far as it would go and rewound her scarf around the lower half of her face. This was better than nothing, but she wished she had a ski mask; it was no good escaping the castle if she was going to be recognized in the village the very next day.

Marcus passed by, clutching an empty bottle.

"All quiet?" he asked. Emily nodded.

"Yeah, it's the same on the other sides; they're just patrolling. We've taken another plank off and fixed it behind the door: had to ram it to get it to stick, but that makes it all the stronger. I've just been doing the icing. Watch your feet on the walkways from now on."

At that moment the police radio emitted a large crackling burst of static. Emily looked out to see the officer talking into the radio and staring toward the car park.

"Something might be up," she said.

"Eh?"

Emily pulled her scarf down. "Something might be up."

"Let's go and see." Together they returned to the entrance lobby, where they met Simon descending from the tower.

"Another car," he said shortly. "And a van. A group's coming this way."

Emily watched several people appear through the gatehouse: they included Marcus's father, now sporting a square white bandage taped to his forehead; Harris, who looked as crabbed as ever; another uniformed officer; and a short woman in a puffed coat and black trousers carrying a bullhorn.

"Negotiations?" Emily said.

"The more the better," Simon muttered. "We should draw it out; gain time."

"What time *is* it?"

"Only twelve-fifteen."

"Hell."

"Look, they're all staying put except that woman. Come on. She's going round the front again."

Back at the pillared room they crowded together in the shadows, eyes fixed on the small area of snow visible from the window. The policeman stationed there had gone. A few moments later the head of the woman came into sight, the bullhorn already at her lips. With a buzz and a whine she switched it on and called out Marcus's name.

"Don't speak to her," Emily cautioned. "Not yet."

The woman waited a moment, then, as if the silence were exactly what she had expected, began to talk slowly and carefully into the bullhorn.

"Hi, Marcus," she said. "I hope you and your friends are listening. My name is Janet and I'm from Norfolk Area Social Services. I've come to talk to you to see if we can't sort things out. First of all, I should say that I am in no way bound to the police—they do not tell me what to do or say, although they have asked me to come here to see you this morning. Nor am I representing your father. I hope that's clear to you. If anything, I am here to act on your behalf—to help you with the issues that concern you. But I need to understand things a bit more, and to do that, I need you to talk to me. I am sure that you are acting for a good reason, and I would very much like to hear from you what that reason is. Do you think you could talk to me, Marcus?"

She lowered the bullhorn and cocked her head, eyes sweeping back and forth along the silent walls.

"What do you think?" Emily hissed.

Marcus shook his head and shivered. "I don't want to talk to her."

After a little, the woman spoke again.

"I'm sure it is difficult for you, Marcus," she said. "But you have to trust me. I'm not asking you to come out, just come to a window." A pause. "I should tell you that I've been given fifteen minutes to make contact with you. If I don't manage to do so, the police will call me away and take matters back into their own hands."

With that she waited. Marcus, Simon, and Emily looked at each other.

"I don't want to talk to her," Marcus said again.

"Better say *something*," Simon said at last. "We've got hours to get through before dusk. We don't want an attack yet if we can help it."

"I agree," said Emily.

Marcus groaned. "But I don't *like* her. She'll twist my words."

"Just tell it how it is. This is a golden opportunity to let them know about your dad. It'll give them something to chew on; maybe take their minds off getting in for a while longer."

Simon nodded. "Time's precious."

"Oh . . . all right. From here?"

"It's as good a place as any."

Marcus gave a heavy sigh and crawled along the deep sill of the window. At its end it narrowed to the same width as the tall, tapering window arch. Marcus squeezed along as far as he could, then craned forward and set his face to the gap, blocking the view of Simon and Emily. The woman spotted him instantly.

"Marcus?" She did not use the bullhorn now.

"Yes." His voice was small and could barely be heard.

"Thank you for coming to talk."

Defiance flared: "We can talk all you want. I'm not coming down."

"Well, talking's good. But to be honest, I don't understand quite why you are up there. Can you help me with it, tell me why you're there?"

"Go on," Emily whispered from behind, as Marcus hesitated.

"You ask my dad," he called. "You ask *him*."

"I will ask him, but I'd rather hear it from you."

"I'm not going back with him. I hate him for what he's done."

"And what has he done, Marcus?"

Again the hesitation. "He's . . . he's . . . look at my face."

"I can't see your face from here, I'm sorry. You're in the shadow. What do you mean?"

"He's . . . I'm not going back with him, that's all."

Behind Marcus, Emily squirmed with frustration. If only he would just get on with it instead of rambling like this! His normal articulateness seemed to have deserted him—he spluttered and coughed and avoided the issue. Perhaps it *was* difficult to denounce your father to the world. But Marcus had told her and Simon easily enough.

The woman spoke up again. "I'm aware there have been problems at home, Marcus," she said. "But these things can usually be worked through, with a bit of help from the outside."

"I don't need help!" Marcus called down. "I've got everything I need in here!"

"What about your friends? Could they speak to me?"

"No! They won't betray me! Stop trying to weasel your way in. I know you've got the police there—and *him*! I've seen them all round the side, lying in wait."

Emily shook her head with suppressed ire. Marcus was doing himself no favors here. *She* could do a better job than this.

"They're not ly—"

"This is my castle! You can wait outside for as long as you want, but you won't get in and I'm not coming out!"

"Okay," the woman said, and the doubt was plain in her voice. "But I still don't quite understand the problem."

"Right—" It was then that Emily acted. She pulled her scarf up over her mouth and nose, and in one swift movement, leaned forward and pulled Marcus forcibly back from the aperture. Ignoring his cry of protest, she thrust herself into his place and crouched down low at the castle window. The woman with the bullhorn looked up at her from the center of the crushed snow. She showed a little surprise, but recovered well.

"Hello," she said.

"Hi," Emily called, lifting the scarf a little so that she could be heard. "I'm a friend of Marcus's."

"Hi. I'm Janet. What's your name?"

Danger. "Er—Katie," Emily said uncertainly, picking a plausible one at random.

"Thank you. Well, Katie, can you tell me what the problem is?"

"Yes," Emily called. "The problem is that Marcus's dad has been hitting him black-and-blue, and we want something done about it. I don't know what excuse he's been giving you, but the truth is that's why Marcus is here and doesn't want to go home, and we think that instead of hounding him you should be arresting his dad instead. That's what the problem is," she said, coming to a halt breathlessly.

The woman seemed taken aback.

"I see. That's a serious accusation." she began.

"You bet it is," Emily said. Her scarf was slipping; she pulled it up.

"We will of course look into it."

"Good."

"But we need Marcus to come out and give a proper statement first. You see that, don't you, Katie? It's no good shouting things out from up there. I can barely hear you, for one thing. Marcus will be quite all right if he comes out. The police will investigate matters thoroughly."

Emily heard Simon give a derisive snort. She cleared her throat.

"Well, can you give us some assurances about what will happen, please?" she called. "Like what will happen to Marcus tonight? Because he doesn't want to go back with his father."

"Everything will be worked through carefully and correctly when Marcus comes down," the woman said blandly. "You needn't worry about him, Katie. You must be feeling very anxious and trapped up there, but it'll be a lot better once you come out, you know. We aren't your enemies."

"That's not quite what I asked," Emily said. *"Can you give us any assurances?* About Marcus and what happens to him. And to his father." It seemed to her that the woman's answer contained nothing concrete whatsoever.

The woman hesitated a little before speaking.

"I can't be sure exactly what will happen, Katie."

"That's not good enough."

They looked at each other for a moment. Then the woman spoke slowly.

"You are being a good friend to Marcus," she said. "At least, you think you are. You're standing by him when he says he is in need, and that's what friends *should* do. But you should ask yourself whether you are doing the right thing encouraging him to lock himself away in a drafty old ruin and not come out to people who have the resources to help him."

"Until I hear some assurance, I think I am," Emily said.

The woman went on as if she had not heard her. "Also, you should ask yourself how well you know him."

Emily's eyes narrowed. "What do you mean?"

"How long have you known Marcus, Katie? Not long, maybe? It's admirable that you should take his word on trust, but—"

"I do more than take his word." In growing anger, Emily saw Marcus's bruised face in her mind's eye. She gestured behind her. "I've got the evidence right here!"

"Even so, are you aware, Katie, that Marcus is a boy with a very fertile imagination?"

"How *dare* you!" Emily felt fury sweep uncontrollably through her. "Forget it! Sod that!" And she pushed herself back from the window and leaped down into the pillared room.

"Katie? . . . Katie?" The woman called up at the empty window. "Are you there? Can you come back? I'm sorry I upset you. . . . Katie? . . . Marcus?" For several minutes more the woman continued to walk back and forth along the strip of wall, calling forlornly through the bullhorn. But there was no answer. The keep was silent. At last she switched the bullhorn off and walked away.

Inside, Emily kicked savagely at the nearest pillar. "That stupid woman!" she cried. "How *insulting*, how *stupid* can you get? She *will* not take your word for it, Marcus! She implied—"

"That's the police for you," Simon said.

"She was Social Services."

"Same thing."

"What a bunch of imbeciles!" Emily was boiling with rage. "I tell you, Marcus, if you went out now, you'd be right back with your father as fast as you could blink."

Marcus seemed very subdued. "Yeah, well, that's why I had to leave home," he said quietly. "I knew I wouldn't get anywhere with them."

"Too right. I was a fool to think I could talk to her."

"No, you did fine. Thanks for trying, Em."

"Yeah, well, moving on . . ." Simon looked at his watch. "Hell, it's still only ten to one. We've got hours before dark yet. They'll try something soon, you can bet on it. What's the weather like?"

"Sky's darkening. Might be another snowstorm coming."

"Let's hope so. Well, all we can do is keep an eye on them. See what they do."

But the pace of the offensive was quickening. From the window of the entrance lobby, they watched the woman with the bullhorn return to the gatehouse and be swallowed up in the growing crowd. All of the people there—policemen, policewomen, officials in suits—looked decidedly cold, and in other circum-stances Emily might have found something funny about the way they huddled together, almost like emperor penguins, shoulders high and arms thrust deep into their pockets. Several of the men were smoking; they stubbed their cigarettes out on the stonework and dropped the butts into the churned snow.

A great consultation now ensued. The woman spoke first, evidently reporting the failure of her mission, and as she finished, half the crowd began to talk at once, all eagerly suggesting how to proceed. The hubbub grew ever more heated until at last the senior officer (Emily suspected he was the one who had spoken to them through the murder-holes) stepped in. He took soundings from different people in turn—another officer, a man in a thick brown overcoat, and the woman with the bullhorn. He even listened briefly to Harris, who kept interrupting with an angry expression on his face. Finally he nodded decisively, unhooked his radio from his jacket, and spoke into it at length. Then he gave a general order, and the group fragmented, most of the police officers heading in both directions around the keep. The woman with the bullhorn remained at the gatehouse, as did Harris, the senior officer and, almost concealed under the arch, Marcus's father. He stood a little apart from the others, slumped against a wall in an attitude of dejection.

"Right, they're doing something." Marcus was agitated. "What is it?"

"Keep calm," Simon said. "They're still waiting.

They're just surrounding the place in case we do a runner."

"He's ordered something up on the radio," Emily hazarded. "What do you think? Ladders?"

"I hope not."

Twenty-five minutes passed before Emily was proved correct. She, Marcus, and Simon spent their time scurrying around the walkways, peering through windows at the besieging forces. They did their best to keep out of sight, but several times Emily was spotted by someone below. One officer caught her eye as she peeped from a latrine window and gave her a derisive mock wave, which made her feel very small and stupid. She ducked back and slunk away, tightening more firmly than ever the scarf that concealed her face.

Since her conversation with the woman, Emily's position on the siege had hardened. She no longer half desired to come to terms with the police, or wished that Marcus would give himself up to their care. The only thing she wanted was to hold out until dark and then escape so that Marcus could fight another day. To this end, she became almost as energetic as Simon.

With the enemy pressing so hard, Simon had now tacitly assumed the role of leader. He was fastest and most untiring in his patrols around the keep and seemed the most clearheaded of all three. His orders were swiftly obeyed. Marcus was stationed up on the tower, where a good view could be had across a wide sweep of the bailey, while Emily was sent running to Marcus's camp to forage any high-energy supplies that could be eaten on the hoof. Simon also improvised some emergency signals, and it was while descending the stairs with a packet of chocolate biscuits that Emily heard three short whistles summoning her immediately to her leader's side. She ran around the walkway, past the kitchen and into the entrance lobby, arriving just as Marcus careered down from the tower. Simon was on his feet by the window, breathing fast.

"This is it," he said tersely. "They've brought the ladders."

A giant red shape had pulled up alongside the flock of small vehicles in the car park. A fire engine. Four members of the fire crew were busy pulling down two long extendable ladders. Emily's heart sank.

"What are we going to do now?" she asked.

"I don't know." Simon's voice was heavy. "There's not much we can do, is there?"

"Knock them off," Marcus said.

"You what?"

"Wait till the men are halfway up, then push the ladders back and away with a stick. We could use a plank for that. They'll be helpless."

"We can't push the ladders away when men are on them."

"Why?"

Simon looked at Marcus. "*But,*" he went on, "we might be able to do it when they first set the ladders against the wall. *Before* anyone gets on them. It's worth a try. Have you got a plank loose down there?"

"There's one that's almost splintered off."

"That'll have to do. Go and get it and bring it back here. No, stop—take it to our entrance hole."

"Why there?"

"That's where we got in; that's where they'll think of getting in, too. Hurry up."

Marcus disappeared down the spiral stairs and Simon turned to Emily. "I was right all along," he said. "He *is* completely mad."

"Wouldn't you be if your dad beat you?"

They watched the ladders' approach. Each was borne by two burly firemen, who carried them slowly across the field along the now well-worn path to the bridge and gatehouse. There they were greeted by the waiting company and given brief orders by the commanding police officer. One of the ladders was sent toward the keep; the other remained where it was. The men laid it down carefully in the snow and stood up again, stretch-ing their arms.

251

"That's odd," Emily said. "Only one . . ."

Simon cursed. "I know what they're doing. They know we're watching; they're going to attack with one and bring the other out when our backs are turned. Hell!"

"We'll have to split forces."

"Yeah. All right, I'll follow this ladder. I'm sure it'll make for our hole. Marcus can help me there. You keep an eye on this one. I'll whistle if we need you."

With that, the leader departed. Emily remained put, watching the gate. She was sure that Simon was right. Although the commanding officer had accompanied the first ladder, taking with him many of the enemy, a small unit of five men had remained behind with the second. They seemed inactive enough for the moment—cigarettes were lit and one man disappeared purposefully around the gatehouse for what she suspected was a pee—but Emily saw them glancing repeatedly at their watches. They were keeping track of the time.

They'll set off shortly she thought. Question is— where will they go?

A shrill cry sounded behind her, then an urgent shout. Despite her orders, she could not resist moving away from the window for a moment and crossing the lobby to the arch that opened out into the empty hall.

On the far side of the open space she could see their entrance hole, with Simon crouched upon its ledge. He was leaning out of the hole, stretching for something.

Down below, Marcus was running into the tower stairway, carrying a long shaft of wood in his hands.

Emily darted back to her window and looked out. The second attack force was still standing in the gatehouse. One man looked at his watch again.

She ran back to the arch. Simon was half sprawled over the stonework. Now Marcus came running along the walkway. She heard him shout, saw Simon draw himself back, saw him grab the shaft of wood. He thrust it out and downward through the hole, extending his arm out as far as possible. He shoved, paused— and raised a fist in triumph; Marcus slapped him on the shoulder.

A distant crash, distant cries.

Emily gave a subdued cheer. She glanced up at the lowering clouds, then at her watch. Just past half one. Time was going so slowly! Hours to go. They hadn't a hope unless the weather helped them. If the visibility went soon, perhaps they could still slip out.

On the far ledge, Simon turned and saw her. She waved and gave the thumbs-up, but he did not return the signal. Instead, he pointed repeatedly behind her with an air of agitation.

Oh—

Quickly, Emily crossed to her window and looked out.

There was no one at the gatehouse. A long, thin indentation in the snow showed where the ladder had once been.

Terror swept through her. Tears welled in her eyes. Where were they? Where had they gone?

Emily forced the swelling panic down and tore herself away from the window. She would look from the tower—that would give her a view along two walls. Ignoring another outbreak of shouts from the far walkway, she raced up the staircase, two steps at a time.

Around and around, gasping for breath . . . Past a cold and empty room, with several arches choked with bird netting. Around and around again . . .

Emily burst onto the roof of the tower. She ran over to the battlements that faced the gatehouse and leaned out until she could see the base of the wall. There was no one on that side of the keep.

She crossed to the next side of the tower and leaned out again, looking to her left. In the distance, close to the far corner tower, people were moving. The ladder in their midst gave off a dull glint. Even as she watched, they seemed to come to a halt.

They were about to create a second point of attack.

As she ran back to the doorway, she saw the first heavy flakes of snow start drifting from the skies.

She pelted down the steps, boots slapping the stones painfully. Out into the entrance lobby and off past the kitchen she ran, without the slightest clue as to what she was about to do.

Onto the walkway. Up to the place where Marcus had left an ice-trap . . . at the last moment she remembered and leaped in midstride. She saw its secretive glint as it passed beneath her, then she was racing on.

Through the arches on the left she glimpsed Simon and Marcus still at their post. They were working in silence now. Simon was still crouching on the broken wall, shoving with the shaft of wood.

Just before the corner tower a small roughly hewn arch opened into the thickness of the outer wall. Emily dashed through, entering a tiny L-shaped room—a latrine, with a hollow seat at its end. Above the privy was a window from which some of the stones had fallen away, leaving a sizable breach in the wall.

It seemed to be in the right position for the group she had seen outside.

Stealthily, Emily crept forward. Almost immediately she heard a muffled clanking from below. They were extending the ladder.

She froze, gazing helplessly at the window ledge,

expecting at any moment to see the ends of the ladder appear in view. Outside, the snow was falling more thickly than before and the sky was a menacing gray. The fields beyond the edge of the woods were growing smudged and indistinct.

Why couldn't you have come an hour ago? she demanded silently of the snow. *It's too late now.*

There was a scraping noise from just below the window ledge and quiet, eager-sounding voices farther down.

Emily snapped herself into action.

She could only think of one, rather ineffectual, thing to do. She took off her bobble hat and stepped over to the window ledge. A thick covering of the previous week's snow lay there. Holding her hat open at the lip of the ledge, she began to scrape the snow into it, cursing whenever the soft hat rim shifted and the falling snow missed its target.

Soft metallic clumping sounds.

Feet ascending the ladder.

Her hands scraped faster. Now she had cleared half the ledge and the hat was full, distorted with the weight of snow.

It would have to do.

Not forgetting to raise the scarf high over her nose, Emily cautiously leaned out over the ledge and looked down. A man was slowly climbing the ladder—a sizable policeman, only a quarter of the way up. Four other men were watching his progress from the drifts below.

Emily squeezed the bulging hat as tightly as she could with her hands, feeling the old crispy snow compress down into a thick ball of ice. It was tempting to take the ice out and spare the hat, but she knew that if she did, there was a chance that the ball might fragment before hitting its target. Instead, she took hold of opposite sides of the hat's soggy rim, pulled them out with all her strength so that they distorted into two thin strips, and tied these together with a single knot.

Then she leaned out again, took careful aim, and flung the woolly ice ball with all her strength at the man on the ladder.

For a split second the ball plummeted. Through the tumbling snowflakes Emily watched the black-and-white zigzag pattern on her hat rotate; she glimpsed the policeman on the ladder looking up, the white face tilting toward her.

The ice ball crashed directly into his face.

A splurge of ice and snow burst from the side of the ball.

The man's head, shoulders, and arms were knocked back by the impact; his hands came away from the ladder. He cried out and fell.

Emily watched in horror.

It took almost no time for him to drop three meters into the drift. The men below were transfixed, except for one supporting the base of the ladder, who launched himself desperately to the side—

The policeman hit the ground.

Deep snow sprayed up and outward as he landed heavily on his back.

Emily bit her lip.

He lay spread-eagled, a dark cross shape scored into the whiteness.

His companions stumbled forward and obscured him. As they knelt, one of them looked upward and shook his fist.

Emily could see a patch of black not far from the man's head—the remains of the hat with which she had dealt the awesome, the undreamed-of blow. She was so shocked that she didn't bother to raise her scarf as it slowly sank down her face and dropped limply around her neck. With round, unblinking eyes she watched as, supported on either side, the man in the snow slowly and painfully raised himself into a sitting position. His helmet was askew, his movements were stiff, but he seemed to be alive and functioning. The deep snowdrift had protected him from the worst of the fall.

With heartfelt relief, Emily let out a pent-up

breath—and even as she did so, she heard three shrill whistles cutting across the wind. *The emergency signal.* It came again, breaking through her daze. They needed her—now.

Tearing herself from the window, Emily ran back onto the walkway and down to the corner tower. Then she was through, speeding along the passage—and in a few more breathless steps was at their side.

Simon stood on the jagged stones, hurling snowballs over the edge. Marcus was feverishly scraping and compacting snow, and tossing each completed ball across to Simon. Both were white-faced and had lost their hats. Their hair was plastered to their scalps. All around them the snow fell with renewed ferocity.

"What can I do?" she gasped.

"More snow!" Marcus could barely speak. His face looked more ghastly than ever, the bruises livid and swollen. He didn't look at her; his fingers were scraping snow from the smallest indentations in the wall.

"They're halfway up!" Simon shouted. He was holding on to a rail for support. "We've knocked the ladder down twice, but they've wedged it this time. Need more snow to keep them off."

Emily started up the walkway toward the next open arch, where a large coating of new snow had accumulated.

"Watch out—the ice!" Marcus's shout came just in time. Emily jerked her foot to the side of another trap and went on. At the arch she knelt and began to gather and compress the snow.

"Chuck it!" Simon yelled. She threw the ball to his waiting hand. Spinning where he stood, he hurled it down into the swirling storm.

"Another!" Time and again they repeated it, Emily scraping her gloves across the stonework until the wool wore through and her fingers were red-raw. The driving snow whipped into her face, her eyes were filmy and could barely see. Time and again she tossed the snowballs to Simon, time and again he sent them whistling into space.

"More!" She could tell by his cry that they were losing the battle, that the attackers were advancing up the ladder, nearer and nearer to the lip of the hole. She knew too that the other window was unguarded now, that enemies would be scaling it, that their hands would be reaching up for the sill, their helmeted heads rising out of the blizzard. She knew it was all over, but still she fought on beside the others in a desperate chain, defending the keep for a final time. Her fingers were bleeding now. The wind was so loud in her ears that she could no longer distinguish Simon's calls from the howls of the gale. She stumbled, knocked her knee against the stonework. A gash, a little blood . . . Ignore it . . . She tossed another snowball over. Now she was so far along the walkway that she had to throw each ball to Marcus, who passed it on to Simon at the hole.

Marcus shouted something. Emily couldn't hear. She shouted back, but her own voice was lost to her.

She scraped another ball together, straightened, and—just as she was about to throw it—stopped dead. The snowball fell from her fingers.

Between two pillars she could see across the driving snow to the walkway on the other side of the hall. At the place where the arch led to the latrine and its window, a dark stooping shape was moving. Its head turned swiftly from side to side.

Midturn, the head froze; it looked directly at Emily.

The enemy had entered the castle.

15

Emily screamed and pointed, and even in the teeth of the gale her cry was loud enough for both Marcus and Simon to hear and understand. Simon leaped down from the ledge. Marcus swiveled, caught sight of the figure on the walkway, and turned, fear etched on his face.

But the figure had seen them too. As Emily watched, it darted to the left, toward the tower, a hefty shape in blue flashing between the columns.

"Run!" she cried. Marcus and Simon came flying down the walkway toward her, Marcus in the lead. He jumped over the ice-trap, and ran on. Simon jumped over the ice-trap, and ran on. Snowflakes whirled about them. Out from the arch that led to the tower raced the dark pursuing figure. Emily could not move for fear.

Marcus and Simon bowled past her. "Come on!" they shouted, but Emily's muscles had turned to water. She edged backward. The enemy came running down the passage through the snow, faster than they were, stronger. She saw his helmet bent toward her like the horn of a beast. His boots pounded the stone, his fists pumped like pistons at his side—

His foot flew sideways out from under him, sending him over with the speed of thought, crashing him onto the stone and ice. He let out a roar of pain that echoed around the empty hall. One leg was twisted, projecting under the railings; his boot hung in thin air. He tried to rise, his hand and elbow slipping in the trap. Behind him another man jumped down from the entrance hole onto the walkway. He saw Emily instantly and began to run, leaping over his fallen comrade.

Emily sped for the staircase. She did not have time to think, she went straight on and down the stairs, too fast to prevent herself from colliding painfully with the curving wall. Her right arm jarred against the stonework as she flew around toward the dark of the storeroom.

Thudding feet came after her, smacking the steps fast as machine-gun fire.

Emily ran through the dimness toward the arch that led into the hall. It was filled with a billowing curtain of snow.

As she reached it, a cry sounded behind her.

"Stop!"

Then she was through and out into the full fury of

the blizzard. Flakes like needles drove into her eyes, spiked her skin from all sides. She was at the bottom of a churning whirlpool of whiteness. The wind tore around and around the hall, scouring the empty husk of the keep, whipping the fallen snow up from the ground so that it bit into her chin and neck. Her scarf was ripped away from her; her hair slapped into her face. She stumbled, then went on as best she could, buffeted first left, then right as she made her way toward what she hoped would be another archway.

She could see nothing. The walls of the keep were merged in with the swirling chaos. A sudden looming shape frightened her, then solidified into the familiar corner of the hut. She dived past it, blinkered and blundering, and collided with gray stone.

Emily glanced back. To her horror a moving form was close behind, driving through the teeth of the storm, one arm outstretched.

In desperation, Emily flung herself forward along the wall, feeling for an opening, expecting every instant a hand to drop upon her shoulder.

The stones ceased; a black space yawned. With a gasp she fell out of the snow into quiet darkness. Instinct told her it was the room with the well—unseen water was dripping all around. Yes, perhaps she could hide here, crouch at the far end. Perhaps he wouldn't see her, perhaps he'd give up and go away.

As fast as she dared, she edged across the uneven floor, making for the back of the room.

From the arch, a scuffle, a step. A man's voice, harsh and angry.

"I see you! Hold it right there."

With a sob, Emily stumbled farther into the blackness. Striding steps pursued her. Her boots tripped on fragments of rubble; she almost fell. Behind her, the footsteps slowed—her enemy was also finding the going hard. Emily's left foot struck something solid, immovable, made of metal. The grille above the well. She rounded its edge and almost immediately came up against a corner of the room.

The way was blocked. She swiveled—and saw the lumbering form approaching through the murk. It had glimpsed her. It came forward with sure purpose. She was trapped, she could not run.

A sudden noise, a cry and crash, and the shape collapsed against the ground. For a moment she stood befuddled, unsure of what had happened. Then she guessed and sprang forward, around where the man sprawled across the grille, his foot trapped between the metal strips; over the rubble, through the dripping columns, across to where the snow blew through the arch; out into the storm.

Now she ran at full tilt, heedless of where she went. For a few strides the blizzard roared around her, then another arch appeared and she was through, across some flagstones and up a flight of spiral stairs.

Shouts came from distant places. They broke into her panic, made her slow at last, her body shaking, her hair wet with sweat and melted snow. Up the stairs she went, straining to catch any significant sound. She did not pause. If she ran straight into the enemy, so be it— but she would not go back down to where the angry shape searched for her, not for anything.

The corner of a familiar room came in sight—the entrance lobby, with its arches leading to the main door and the pillared room. It was empty, but there were voices not far off and a recurrent banging.

Where could she go? Where could she hide?

From here she had several options: main entrance, pillared room, kitchen, walkway, tower. The tower and kitchen were dead ends, the entrance was blocked, the other two ways led to where the enemy had gotten in.

Was that a sound below her on the stairs?

Emily made up her mind. Without bothering with stealth, she climbed the last few steps and entered the lobby. The banging sound was coming from the entrance stairs—someone was unbarring the door so that the main force could get in. Emily ignored both this and the way to the pillared room. She ignored the way up to the tower.

Without hesitation she crossed the lobby and went through the arch into the kitchen.

Emily crouched by the third and smallest of the ovens in the kitchen wall. It was at floor level and resembled the opening of a large brick-lined drain. The inside was lined with dark red tiles.

Hunching her shoulders, clenching her fists, Emily crawled swiftly into the oven. She went as fast as she could, supporting her front half on her elbows and ignoring the pain from her gashed knee. Her shoulders passed in easily, but her hips were a tighter squeeze. As she wriggled, she thought of the witch from *Hansel and Gretel*, who had crawled into an oven in similar fashion and been burned to death. With that, she gave a final push, and her hips passed through the gap.

Once in, the oven was surprisingly roomy—big enough for her to turn and adopt a sitting position. The interior was formed of tiles wedged in end-on. It was domed, with a ledge running around it about halfway up. Emily adjusted herself until she was sitting as far away from the opening as possible, with her legs hunched up tightly and her back flat against the front wall of the oven.

Then she rested and listened.

For a while she heard little except the wind. Several pairs of footsteps passed the kitchen arch, but to Emily's relief, none of them came inside.

Unknown time passed. Emily tried to read her watch, but it was too dark in the oven to make out its face. The light faded. Suddenly she stiffened, her heart jolted. Footsteps were entering the kitchen.

"Better check these," a woman's voice said.

"Get a move on, then." A man's voice, surly and dispirited.

"Have you got your flashlight?"

"'Course not! Didn't think we'd be grubbing about in holes, did I?" As he spoke, the man was evidently kneeling to look into one of the ovens. There was a hollow tang to his voice when he next spoke. "Can't see a bloody thing. It's empty, though."

"How do you know that if you can't see?"

"They're not in here, they've got out somehow."

"This one's empty too. Try the last one."

"They've got out somehow."

"He said there was no other way."

"If you believe that crusty old git you'll believe anything." The voice was coming closer. "There's some hole he's not noticed, that's all."

Emily crouched in the darkness. A scuffle directly

outside her oven. A presence in the opening. If he stuck his head through, he had her.

"There's no one here."

"Are you looking?"

She saw from the corner of her eye the brief vapor of his breath, smelled mint from the sweet he was suck-ing. A nerve in her cheek twitched.

"Come off it! This is the smallest one of all. It's empty."

"Let's go, then."

The presence withdrew. More scuffling outside. Emily's cheek twitched again.

"Where now?" the man's voice asked.

"Stay on this level," the woman replied wearily. "That's what they said. We go round again."

"Oh, *great*. It's a complete—hey, did you hear that?"

Emily had heard it, a yell of savage triumph echoing around the castle. It stabbed her through the heart.

"They've got one! Let's go and see."

"No, I told you. We stay on this level."

Still bickering, the voices receded and Emily was left in the solitude of her oven, staring dry-eyed into the dark. The echo of the cry resounded in her head. *They've got one. They've got one.* Something inside her seemed to shrivel up and die. Never before had she felt quite so defeated and forlorn.

Running feet passed the kitchen. She heard more

calls and the crackle of a radio. Somewhere far off a man laughed.

Part of Emily knew that it was now time to give up; that since one of them had been caught, her identity would soon become known, no matter how long she remained hidden. But another, greater part of her was more stubborn. It refused to surrender meekly, and the sounds of their enemies tramping through their castle made it cold with rage. It would not give in until she was wrenched bodily from her hiding place, like a snail pulled from its shell on the tip of a pin.

Or until she made good her escape.

This would be Emily's last act of defiance. Even now they would be interrogating their captive; even now they might know who she was. But even if they were waiting for her when she got home (she had a brief, shuddering flash in her mind's eye of them sitting on the sofa, her parents behind them, grim and silent), it was better that than being caught skulking like a rat in the bowels of the castle. Besides, there was even the small possibility that her friends wouldn't welsh on her, that the enemy would never find her out. . . .

Emily thrust the engaging thought abruptly from her head. Come off it—there was no real chance of that. But escape from the castle *was* possible. With dusk falling fast she might yet get out unseen.

Wriggling herself around, she crouched just inside the oven opening and peered out. From what little she could see, she guessed that it must be nearly twilight. The kitchen was very dark. It was impossible to tell if it was still snowing outside, but the sound of the wind had lessened. Squinting at her watch, she made out the time: only 3:50, still not officially dusk. But it would not be much longer. She would wait a little, then make her break.

All was quiet. Gaining a little confidence, Emily extended her head through the opening and peeped cautiously toward the lobby. At first there was nothing to see except varying swathes of shadow, but suddenly a faint yellow light began to appear on the far wall. The light grew stronger, moving up and down in time to the owner's flashlight. Emily retreated out of sight just as two sets of footsteps entered the lobby.

"All right," a voice said, and Emily recognized it immediately as belonging to the senior policeman. "We'll wait here." The voice still sounded calm and gentle, but it was now also regretful and tired.

"Why?" At the sound of this single, sullen word, Emily clenched her fingers against the tiles. It was Simon.

"Because someone's coming up to escort you to the car. I can't spare anyone here since they're too busy looking for your friends. Are you *sure* you don't know where they're hiding?" Tired, regretful, reasonable.

"Not a clue."

"But you know how many there are?" (Silence.) "We know there are at least two more of you, Marcus and Katie. Anyone else?"

Simon did not reply.

"Well, it doesn't matter. We're bringing searchlights in shortly. Oh, yes, we're pulling out the stops for you lot. We've got all the emergency services of West Norfolk catching cold in this godforsaken ruin on your account, laddie, people who would have been better employed doing their proper jobs elsewhere. What did you think you were up to, playing silly buggers like this? You ought to be ashamed, wasting everyone's time."

"We were not wasting time!" Simon cried. "You wait till you see Marcus's face, just wait! Then you'll see why he didn't want to go home! None of you give a toss what's happened to him—you're the ones who should be ashamed!"

"What did he tell you, then?" The policeman spoke so quietly that Emily could barely hear him, and it had the effect of calming Simon also.

"We spent a night here," he said in a subdued voice. "Not doing any harm. But Marcus was late getting back, and his dad was waiting for him. Beat him up—but don't take my word for it, you'll see for yourself! Oh, and smashed his bicycle up too. You'll find the bits in his garden, *if* you're interested. That's why Marcus decided to run off. He was crazy to come here, I think, but I don't blame him for wanting to get away. That's all. You'll hear it better from Marcus when you find him."

In the oven Emily nodded grimly. Nice one, Simon.

"I'm sure I will. Where *is* Thomson? He can't have got lost, surely." Emily could hear a single set of footsteps circling the lobby. "The thing is, lad, I've already seen that bike of Marcus's. His father showed it to me when I went over."

"Well, then, you've seen—"

"I've seen it padlocked to the garden fence, good as new. Well, one of the handlebars is a bit bent, but that's only to be expected. Marcus is a bit of a careless cyclist apparently, always coming off it in some dramatic fashion. Like he did only the other day."

"You're not telling me—"

"Skidded on the ice while taking a corner too fast. He went right off into the side of a car. Knocked his face quite badly, I understand."

"His dad told you that! And you believe him! My God!" Simon's voice was shrill with fury and indignation.

"I'm sure we could get witnesses if it came to it, lad. He did it quite publicly, you see, not down some back alley. On one of the roads leading into the market square in King's Lynn it was, a couple of days ago. He was lucky he didn't have to go to hospital."

He waited, as if wondering whether Simon wanted to say anything. In the oven, Emily could hear her heart pounding in her chest. Lies! All lies!

"As I say, it's not the first time Marcus has had some reckless accident like that," the policeman went on. "He's come to our attention before. He's always going off without permission, often hurting himself, too, one way or another. Small wonder his father locked up his bike and forbade him to go out again, but this didn't stop young Marcus. The next thing his dad knew, he'd bolted."

"I don't believe you," Simon said, but his voice was tinny and hollow, lacking all conviction.

"Doesn't matter much what you believe now, does it? If you'd had the wit to contact us properly, all this trouble would have been avoided. Still, Marcus does have a reputation for being rather plausible, so it's not altogether surprising he fooled you. Ah—here he is. What happened to you, Thomson? You're late."

"Sorry, sir; got a bit lost."

"*Really*, Thomson. All right. Here's one for your

charge. I don't think he's going to cause you any grief. Are you, lad?"

"No." Simon's voice was barely audible.

"No. Any sign of the searchlights, Thomson?"

"On their way, sir."

"All right, off you go."

Two sets of footsteps departed. One set remained, pacing around the lobby. As if in a dream, Emily heard the crackle of the radio and the man speaking into it. She was visualizing Simon being led downstairs, visualizing the look on his face. She imagined what he would be thinking. And as she did so, the words of the policeman were battering against her skull. *Skidded on the ice; knocked his face quite badly . . .* For a few moments, facts that had seemed incontrovertible began to slide into doubt and suspicion. She and Simon had taken Marcus's account on trust. Had he—?

No. Emily thrust the doubts away. *Of course* the father would come up with a story like that, *of course* he'd invent a cock-and-bull version to fool the police. And being fools they'd fallen for it, unquestioningly. It was hopeless attempting to convince them. Marcus had been right to run. All she could do now was try to escape and hope Marcus did too.

A new set of boots passed the kitchen. Instinctively, Emily wormed her way back a little.

"No luck, Hatchard?"

"Afraid not, sir. No more up the chimney. We've looked in every corner we can. I'm pretty sure the ground and first floors are clear, although the weather hasn't helped us."

"Okay. I want all the rooms on the second floor checked. There's only a couple you can officially get into, but there are these others, look, which they might have got access to. Along a ledge or through some broken bars. These ones, for instance." Emily could hear paper being folded.

"They look pretty inaccessible."

"The whole bloody castle's meant to be inaccessible, Hatchard. You'll find them both together I expect."

"Just two of them, sir?"

"There's no evidence of any others, no matter what PC Jones says. Just two."

The voices moved off and Emily heard them no more. Immediately, to quell the confusion in her head, she began counting steadily under her breath. It was too dark now to see the time, so she counted the seconds off, one by one, in groups of sixty. When she had done this fifteen times she would make her break for it, come what may. Fifteen minutes would give the searchers ample time to get stuck in the upper floors. And it would then be fully dark.

For the first five of her sixty-second counts there was a great deal of movement close by, especially in the entrance lobby. Heavy equipment, presumably search-lights, was being brought in; orders were given; people moved up and down the spiral stairs, and in ones and twos set off toward the other towers. Several times, torches hoovered up the darkness nearby, but no one double-checked the kitchen.

For the second five minutes all was much quieter. Emily crouched in readiness like an animal in its lair. As she counted down through the last five, she began to shiver with fear and expectation. Three minutes to go. . . . Doubts assailed her. Why bother trying? It was hopeless. She would never make it. It was a thousand to one against.

Two minutes to go. . . . No—be strong. It would take no time at all to get to the entrance hole and uncoil the rope. No time at all. Then she would be down and off over the snow, like Simon had said.

One minute to go. . . . She imagined Simon being led away . . . Leaving only her and Marcus. Marcus . . . She saw his battered face before her. He'd said . . .

Time's up.

She did not allow herself to hesitate—she knew that if she did so she would never go at all. Taking a deep breath, she ducked her head and shoulders through the narrow opening. A quick look toward the entrance lobby, the most dangerous place in the castle, and then the rest of her followed, wriggling like a worm, until— heart hammering, breathing heavily—she crouched freely in the darkness of the kitchen.

Without a pause she tiptoed toward the arch that led to the lobby. On her left a few desultory snowflakes dribbled in through the door to the hall. Night had fallen now, and had it not been for a powerful search-light in operation somewhere above, Emily would have been unable to see her hand in front of her face. The reflected light showed dimly on the opposite sides of the hall. The great fireplace was a black crescent mid-way up the wall.

Emily looked along the walkway. The route to the next tower was clear. So far, so good. She pulled her hood over her head, then—crouching as low as possible and hugging the wall farthest away from the open arches— she set off down the walkway as softly as a ghost.

She remembered Marcus's ice-trap only as her foot slipped away from under her. The next instant, she was hitting the floor, unable to suppress a gasp of agony— which must have echoed around the entire keep. For a second, she lay panting on the floor, waiting for the light to sweep down and hit her.

Then, frantically, she tried to rise, slipping repeatedly on the ice.

Bloody Marcus . . . It's all his fault. Everything.

She was upright again. Okay. Step over the ice, back on firm ground. . . . So far, so good. . . .

A great cry echoed through the castle.

"There!"

Emily ran for her life.

"Lights, bring the lights!"

Commotion erupted all around the keep, people calling, boots running, lights swirling like sparklers past windows and arches. A great yellow beam swung across the open hall. Unseen crows burst from their nests and flew croaking into the black sky. And among it all, Emily reached the corner tower, passed through it like the wind, and was on the other walkway, approaching the ruined stretch of wall.

The searchlight appeared to have lost her; she reached the entrance hole in darkness. Right—the rope, where was the rope? Her fumbling fingers stubbed themselves repeatedly across the railings and the snowy ledge. She had so little time—in a moment they would be on her. . . . There! She had it, sodden, coiled, caked with snow. Still tied to the rail. Exerting all her strength, Emily picked up the rope and hurled it out into space. The slap it made as it hit the wall below was almost drowned by another wave of shouts behind her.

Sobbing with fear, Emily scrambled onto the ledge, grasped the rope, and slipped under the rail, ready to make the descent. And still they didn't show up, no lights, no policemen, nothing.

She was going to make it; she was going to get out.

Then, as she stood on the lip of the wall, ready to lower herself into the safety of the darkness, she saw why they hadn't come.

She took it all in at a glance. Through the arch opposite, across the shadowy expanse of the great hall, she could see the tallest of the towers, two full stories above her. The top of the tower was spotlit by many lights, and a crowd of people stood upon it. They were all staring in one direction, at a point a little way along the dilapidated battlements that extended out from the side of the tower. They could not get onto the battlements from the tower itself without crossing a high guardrail; and they could not cross the guardrail for fear of alarming the thin figure who stood, bathed in searchlights, on an outcrop of crumbling stone. He was gesticulating wildly. The crowd on the tower had fallen silent.

Emily could guess what Marcus was saying from the way he kept pointing off into the darkness beyond the wall. It was a precarious position; the stone on which he stood was right at the end of the existing battle-ments. Behind him the lights illuminated a few broken stumps, but most of the wall had crumbled to the level of the next story down. A black hole marked where the ceiling of the room below had fallen away.

Marcus was cornered. He could not go anywhere. Alive, that is.

He was threatening to jump.

At this thought a great anger filled Emily, directed at Marcus's stubbornness, his willful stupidity. *Go ahead, then, jump!* See if she cared. If he didn't want to work things out sensibly, if he wanted to go on following his harebrained schemes instead of confronting his trouble head-on, then let him fall! She was going home for a bath and a meal. She might as well smell good when the police came calling.

Marcus had got himself into this mess. If it hadn't been for him they would never have thought to enter the keep in the first place, and she, Emily, would never have had the notion of spending the night inside. It was all his fault! They would never have been surrounded by dozens of police, as well as goodness knows how many firemen, social workers, and other hangers-on. There was probably a reporter outside the entrance right now. If it had not been for Marcus, the worst that might have happened to Emily was Harris collaring her for sledding. How mild that would have been!

Without Marcus nothing would have happened. But it was his father's brutality that made him act this way, whatever that stupid policeman said. *Skidded on the ice*— how lame was that? Marcus had been forced to run—and now, inevitably, he had been caught. He was more cornered than ever, surrounded, besieged.

She took another look at the lone figure on the battlements. He was crouching now, probably weary, and with every strong gust of wind he swayed a little. The people in the tower were talking to him again—no doubt a mixed bag of promises, pleas, and reassurances—and suddenly, in a moment of cold clarity, Emily realized that he would give in to none of them. He was cornered, helpless, but this did not mean he would surrender. There was simply too much pride in him.

He would not give up. He really would jump instead. He was that stupid.

Emily's hands were sore from gripping the rope so tightly. She stood on the ledge, with escape a couple of minutes away. On the other side of the castle, Marcus sat on a small lump of stone, death on either side. They would never talk him down. They did not speak the right language. Marcus was besieged, immune to their reasonable tones, their careful promises of support. He would jump or fall.

Emily felt a rushing in her head. She could not leave him. She knew him better than they did. Numbly, hand over hand, she pulled herself forward across the ledge to the railing. Then she ducked under it and dropped back into the castle. Without bothering to hide herself, she walked slowly back the way she had come.

When she was almost at the lobby a sudden noise alerted her to danger. Pressing into the shadows, she saw a crowd of people come spilling down the spiral staircase. Except for their footfalls, they were silent. They crossed the room and disappeared. For a moment Emily was nonplussed, but then she guessed the reason.

"They're clearing out," she thought. "Trying to take the pressure off him."

When the exodus had finished, Emily continued on into the lobby. Muffled voices from above indicated that not everyone had gone—negotiations with Marcus were still taking place. She could distinguish his voice occasionally, louder and more strident than the low mumble of the negotiator. He didn't seem to be calming down.

Emily climbed the spiral staircase for the final time, up to the room on the second floor, directly below the roof of the tower. It was a place she had not investigated properly before. Someone had left a large metal lamp leaning against the wall beside the stairwell. It carved the room in two, throwing a bright yellow light against the ceiling and opposite wall, while leaving the rest in shadow. There had once been four ways out of the room. Three were blocked with railings and bird netting, but the fourth arch, although pitch black, was open.

Marcus's voice sounded clearly through this arch, and Emily began to detect snatches of what he said: ". . . as I come out you'll lock me up, I'm not a fool . . . I took possession and by rights it's mine . . . when you broke in you got what was coming . . ." He was speaking too fast, the words tumbling out all over each other. Emily hastened her pace, crossed the room, and looked through the arch. Beyond was a narrow passage that had perhaps once led to a balcony running around the hall. For the first few meters it was dark and roofed, but after that the ceiling ended abruptly and the upper portions of the passage were flooded with light from above. Emily realized she was directly below the battlements on which Marcus stood.

She walked a little distance along the passage until she stepped into the open air. Thick snow crunched under her feet. The harsh white light picked out the ruined walls on either side, lower now and fractured, ending in a mess of flint and ice. A little farther on, the floor of the passage itself became unsafe and railings barred the way. The stonework beyond was smothered with grasses poking through the snow.

Emily turned around and looked up. Marcus was framed against the sky, like a gargoyle spotlit from the side. He was crouching awkwardly, hands gripping the rough stone of the battlement beside his feet. His hood was hanging torn and loose, and his hair was matted and wild; a patch just over his temple was thick with something dark. He was gazing at the floor and much of his face was in shadow. Someone farther off was talking to him—low, calming words—and with a jolt Emily realized that she had heard the voice before. It was a man, but it was not the police officer who spoke—it was Marcus's father.

"—you don't want to be here," the voice was saying. "None of us do. Come down and we'll talk things over."

"Go away." Marcus's voice was barely recognizable. "I don't want to speak to you. I don't want to see you. Keep back or I'll do it! I will!"

"If you come down, you won't have to see me, I promise. I'll keep well away— Just as long as I know you're safe, I'll be happy."

In the darkness below, Emily gritted her teeth. The

hypocrisy of the man was sickening! His wheedling sounded almost convincing; you'd almost believe he cared. But it would have no effect on Marcus now. She feared for him. Without raising her voice, so that she did not attract anyone else's attention, she whispered urgently upward.

"Marcus!"

No good. He was turned away from her, he could not hear. She was too far down, invisible below. Emily considered the walls. The inner one was low, only a little above waist height, but ahead it rose sharply. It was about a meter wide; this thickness was all that separated her from a hideous two-story plummet to the bottom of the hall. It was also caked with snow and ice.

In doubt, Emily checked on Marcus again. He was gently swaying, utterly worn out. She cursed—he would not be thinking straight. He was going to do it, she knew he was. *Unless . . .*

Clumsily, she hoisted her leg onto the wall, then rolled herself bodily onto the stones. The deep snow wet her face and soaked instantly through her jeans. With great care she got on all fours, trying not to notice the black emptiness at her side, and began to inch her way up the steeply angling masonry.

Up in the light, the father was still spinning his lies.

"How many times do I need to say sorry? I know

I've been mad when you've gone off, but you worry me, that's all. I don't want anything to happen—"

"Yeah, right. You just want to lock me up; you restrict everything I do—"

"No, I don't! And even if I did, it works both ways, Marcus. You've hurt me too."

A little way below, Emily made a face of disbelief. He was absolutely shameless! Flint ends were stabbing her palms and pricking her through her jeans with every shuffle forward. She could not go any faster—the rubble steepened here—but if she got a little higher she might make herself heard.

Marcus was sneering now. "Hurt you? Oh, yes? How?"

The voice hesitated, then went on. "We've both found it hard, since your mother—"

"*How* did I hurt you?"

"Well, those things you said about me."

"I didn't say anything!"

"About your face—that I did that . . ."

"So? You did! Sort of."

"Marcus—"

"If I hadn't been so scared of you I wouldn't have been coming back so fast, would I? I'd have been more careful. But I was worried—I wasn't concentrating at that corner. That's why I slipped. See? It *is* your fault."

"That's not the same as hitting you, Marcus. . . ."

"Yeah, well. It's as good as."

Emily had stopped climbing. Her face was pressed against the snow. She felt as if she had been punched in the stomach—all breath had been driven out of her. She thought she would vomit.

He *had* lied. The policeman had been right. Marcus had made it up. The face, the beating, everything. Lies . . . all lies.

Whether he had been driven more by his love for the castle or his hatred of his father, she didn't know or care. Here she was, hanging on to a crumbling wall, risking her neck for his. It made her head swim. All this—all this mess was his work and his alone! It was his tissue of lies and half-truths, his mix of history and invention that had lured them in and kept them there. His stories that had won them over, time and time again, no matter how ludicrous they seemed. They were fools, both of them—Simon, now speeding through the dark in a police car; Emily, stretched out in the snow at the top of a ruin. Utter fools. And Marcus had brought them both low.

As she lay there, the conversation intruded again on her despair.

"We shouldn't argue about that, son. No one's interested in who said what. We just want you down."

"Tough." To Emily his voice now sounded like a sulky child's.

"What beats me is why you're here at all. What's this place do for you, anyway?"

Marcus said nothing.

"Good for games, is that it? Good for playing games?"

"Games? Yeah, you *would* think that."

"So why d'you come here, then? I just don't get it, son, I don't understand."

Marcus did not answer immediately, and when he did so, his voice was sullen and hesitant. "It gives me something. It makes me feel . . ." He came to a halt; started again. "It's . . . it's better than being out there, that's all," he said. "There's nothing for me out there. Nothing."

There was a baffled silence. "What sort of answer's that, Marcus?" The voice carried a note of irritation. "You're not making sense. Your mother said you were a clever boy. What d'you think she'd say if she heard you now?"

This roused Marcus at last. "How the hell would you know what she'd say?" he shouted. "Get lost!"

His father gave a cry of exasperation. "Right, I've had enough of this nonsense. We all have. I'm coming to take you down."

Emily heard a scuffling and a despairing shout from Marcus.

"No! Get back! I'll jump if you come any closer!"

Quiet voices spoke urgently to the father, and the scuffling noise stopped dead. Silence fell; the father did not speak again.

Emily stole a look over her shoulder. Marcus was half standing on his stump of stone, the harsh light picking out the despair upon his face. At this, all Emily's furious thoughts of climbing down and leaving him fell away, leaving behind a calm resolve.

Liar or not, she knew what he needed to hear, and no one else did. She had to go on.

Slowly, painfully, she drew herself farther along the jagged stones, and in a few moments broke upward into the light. With tortuous care, she rotated so that her back was pressing against the stonework, and Marcus was in full view.

She was level with the floor of the battlements now, still below Marcus but high enough to see across to the roof of the tower. Three people stood there. It was hard to make them out amid the glare of the spotlights, but one was the father, another the chief police officer. They had just noticed her. Someone called something; Emily ignored it, but Marcus heard and looked slowly in her direction.

"All right, Marcus," she said softly.

There was blood on his temple and his face was white and puffy. As he turned, his eyes went into shadow.

"Em!" His voice was hoarse, but sounded pleased. "I thought they'd got you long ago."

"Nope." She was unsure how to judge it, what tone to give him. "Nope, they never found me."

"Nice one. Where were you?"

"In an oven."

She heard him laugh softly. "No way! That's better than the chimney." His voice fell. "Simon's gone, though, I heard him."

"Yeah."

"They smelled the smoke, Em. I was so cold I had a cig. They smelled it like you said they would. Came looking." A thought struck him. "Why've you come up here, Em? You could have got out, maybe."

"Because I saw you. I came to help."

"That's kind, but there's nothing we can do now. The castle's fallen. It's all over."

His head was resting on his knee and his voice was so muffled and listless that she could barely hear him.

"We should come down now, Marcus," she said. "We should walk out of here together."

"What for? They keep telling me stuff, but I just

can't make it real. Not real like this was. Dad's here, you know; he wants me back too, he says. They promise all sorts of things—but it's funny, I can't see how any of it will actually work for me. I don't know. I can't be bothered with it all, Em. I'm tired. Everything's so dreary."

"It doesn't have to be. Maybe you've just got to believe them. . . ."

His voice sharpened instantly. "Why should I? For that matter why should I believe *you*?" His head lifted off his knee, his hidden eyes bored into her. "They haven't sent you here, have they? Told you what to say?"

"Don't be stupid! You think I'd turn traitor now after all this, after all we've gone through?" She had been keeping her anger under strict control; here it burst out a little, but even as she spoke she realized that she was now adopting the kind of language Marcus understood. He shrugged, somewhat mollified.

"Maybe," he said grudgingly. "Yeah, fair enough, I trust you. But it's all slipping away, Em. I was trying to say to Dad, before you got up here, about the castle, about what it meant. They all asked me what we were doing, what we wanted. And the stupid thing was that I couldn't say. . . . I couldn't articulate it so that they understood. Maybe it was the lights, or seeing Dad, I don't know, but I couldn't concentrate. I sounded like a fool. Well . . ."

He gazed off into the darkness, perhaps looking out at distant, unknown houselights. "It's all over for us here," he said, "and you know there's nothing for me out there. So I decided I'd . . . but it's a long way . . . and I haven't done it yet."

In the shadows of the passage below her, Emily saw a movement. One of the watchers from the tower had come down to prevent her escape. Perhaps fearing that she too would threaten to jump, the shape hung back almost out of sight. She ignored it, kept her eyes fixed on Marcus.

"If you do that," she said loudly, "you're going to miss the best bit of all."

The hunched figure on the battlement glanced at her again. "Which is what?" Marcus asked.

"You think they can keep this quiet now?" Emily spoke with new assertion. She knew now what she was going to say. "After all the people they've had to bring in from round the county to flush us out? Three of us, Marcus—that's all, don't forget—just three of us have withstood this siege all day. They came in the morning, and we took whatever they could throw at us till nightfall. You think they'll be able to keep that quiet? I don't think so. It'll be all over the papers tomorrow—

and not just the local ones, either. All of them. Why? Because there's never been a story like this!"

"Not for hundreds of years, here," he said, fingering the stone.

"Or anywhere. Not just here, Marcus. Anywhere. This is better than those stories they write up in those old guidebooks, and you know it. Think about you and Simon for a start. How long did he keep firing at them, pinning the main army down? Must have been half an hour—you and him, side by side against dozens. And they couldn't break in there until you were attacked from the back! They never got past you, Marcus, think of that."

She was watching him closely, saw him nod.

"And the other thing is," she went on breathlessly, following up her advantage, "the other thing is that you don't even know the full story yourself! What about my side of it? You haven't heard what I did during the siege. While you and Simon were busy, I held off a second troop of them from my window. I sent six of them tumbling off the ladder by tipping hatfuls of snow down on their heads! Arse over tit they all went—you should have seen it! Headfirst into the drifts, six pairs of blue legs wriggling! Want to read about that in the papers tomorrow? You ought to."

Emily was warming to her theme now, revving up

her imagination nicely. "And did you see those two blokes upended in your ice-trap? No? I did. They nearly went over the edge; it was great! A policeman and a fireman, side by side, hanging on by their finger-tips. *And* there was the one I trapped down the well— he regretted chasing me, I can tell you. . . . Don't say you're giving up before you hear all this!"

Emily wheezed to a halt, totally out of breath.

"The well? Really?" Marcus said.

"What I'm saying," Emily said, "is that after a fight like this there's nothing dishonorable about surrender-ing when you're down to your last two men. What *is* dishonorable is running away from the enemy, which is why I didn't escape when I had the chance. And that's just what you'd be doing if you take a nosedive off."

She finished. Marcus crouched where he was, his face in shadow. Emily flicked a look at the figures on the tower, but the lights were too bright and she could not make them out.

"You're right, Em." Marcus dropped first one leg, then the other, over the stone and pushed himself off, landing in the snow on the edge of the battlement. "It was weird, you know. I'd lost it for a moment, I couldn't see what it was we'd been up to—I'm sure it was the lights that did it. But you're right. What we did was better than anything that's gone before, at least since Hugh was here. We can tell—"

A dark shape reared up behind Marcus, covering him with shadow. Light glinted around its edge as it sprang to secure him. Emily cried out. Marcus half turned, flinched back from the figure, and lost his balance. His foot scrabbled for an instant on the edge of the battlement, then he toppled sideways. The policeman made a grab at thin air. Marcus disappeared without a sound into the well of darkness, followed by tumbling fragments of snow.

There was a dull sound from the passage floor.

Several people cried out. Emily screamed. She scrambled a little way down the edge of the wall, then jumped bodily into the passage, landing heavily on her feet.

Marcus lay on his back, eyes closed, one arm bent oddly underneath him. The woman had run from the passage and was bending at his side, but Emily shoved past her and crouched beside his head.

"Marcus!"

He opened his eyes. "People are always interrupting me, Em. You should be used to it." His voice was faint, but he gave her the old grin.

"Don't try to move," she said.

"I didn't know you could tell a story so well. You certainly won me over."

Emily couldn't help herself then. The question boiled up within her. "That stuff about your dad. Why say it, Marcus? Why make it up?"

A slight expression of doubt passed across his face.

"I don't know, Em." He frowned. "It just sounded better that way somehow. More real, more impressive. It gave me a reason . . ."

She waited for more, but his mind had moved on. "Em—did someone really fall down the well?"

"No. I lied."

"Oh. Thought it was too good to be true." His eyes closed, then opened again.

"Do you think the papers will take a firsthand account?" He shifted a little. "Ah, my arm—! I mean, I mean, we don't want them to get it wrong."

"We'll worry about that later. Stay still. And don't move your arm."

Marcus seemed satisfied. He closed his eyes. Emily stayed sitting in the snow beside him. She could hear a voice on a radio somewhere and footsteps moving up through the empty rooms of the castle.

"Are you all right, Katie?" a voice at her shoulder asked.

She didn't look up.

"It's Emily," she said.